Sunrise Reprise
An Emoticon Fable

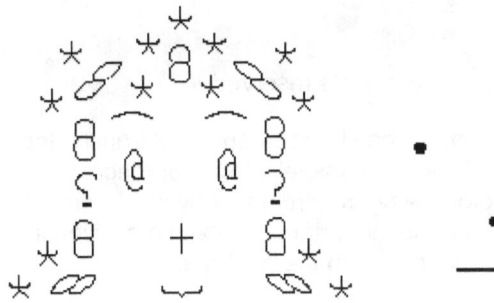

Story and Drawings

by

Robert Yoshibo Shell

Robert Yoshibo Shell
Sørkedalsveien 230
0754 Oslo, Norway

ISBN: 978-82-998265-1-8

Printed by Createspace
www.createspace.com

DEDICATION

To Reiko, in loving memory

CONTENTS

FORWARD

A long long time ago, in an era far far away, I received a text message for the first time with the now familiar notation – a colon followed by a single parenthetical punctuation mark, signifying an emoticon. I immediately saw a character in a work of fiction. That character slowly transformed himself into Les Dan Nil. And this is his story, told by a narrator drifting towards death out in the open sea.

1   WITHOUT THE I

It was my fifth day at sea without food. Fourth day without water. Third day without wind. I lay in the one-man skiff, baking in the unforgiving heat. I used the dismantled jib sail as a protective cover to shield me from the searing sun. From time to time I caught myself sucking on an empty plastic gallon jug. I knew there was no water. But that didn't stop me from trying to extract a drop or two as if by some miracle, the jug had refilled itself. Obviously the act of a mindless mind.

It was a mind that wandered aimlessly beyond the boundaries of my sense of self, as if it had a life of its own. My mind looked back at myself, like a superior clinical observer watching a simple life form through a microscope. That looked-at-self took offense confronting the audacity of the looking-self, having no answer to its questioning watch.

Clearly the observer was breaking ties with me. It no longer wanted to ally itself with me. I had lost its trust. And who would I become once that tie between the observer and observed was severed? Where would the "I" exist? I would be without my "I." Stuck in the vicious circle of my in-between self, chasing the receding definition of my identity, I had no answers.

The only answer I could muster? Hunger was my name. Thirst was my identity. Suffering my only awareness. Pain the sum total of my entity. I was nothing more than a barely breathing, blinking, dehydrating body of flesh impersonating some semblance of a life form at the lowest level. I may as well have been nameless. What was the point of having a name? It had no value whatsoever in that deserted open sea.

There was a time when my name did mean something. It had a recognition factor. I was somebody--a child star of a hit sit-com. Everyone knew my name. It was a household word. I was pampered by photo shoots, interviews, award ceremonies, guest appearances. I was an Emmy nominee!

Then it all fell apart. While shooting the fourth season, one of my co-stars suddenly died. Another had to go into rehab. A third co-star was dropped from the cast when negotiations broke down in her demand for a salary raise. My character was the ballast for the show but nothing ever clicked with the replacement cast. The chemistry never sparkled. The flawed storyline to fit the new characters caused the bottom to fall out of the show's ratings. And I became an unemployed actor at the ripe old age of ten.

Before I hit my teens, my nest egg dried up, thanks to my parents' mismanagement of my earnings through tax evasion and involvement in a Ponzi scheme. That put my father in prison and my mother on alcohol and welfare. So it was, from anonymity to instant stardom and back to anonymity, and dire poverty, as I entered adolescence, full of rage at my parents and the cruelty of life. Upon graduation I abandoned my mother like a thief in the night.

Eventually I found myself in the Bahamas crewing as a go-fer slash dish-washer on a sloop. One night, I decided I had had enough of my dismal life, and stole a rental skiff at a resort to stage my disappearance. I imagined a mysterious and romantic death, the Amelia Earhart /Antoine de St. Exupery way. Of course they were both aviators which I was not. Nor was I even a true sailor. But I knew enough to get me to the nowhere part of the sea.

That romantic dream of death at sea remained alive while the wind filled the sails. But when the sails went limp, not just for an afternoon, or even a day, but three days, the romance disappeared beyond the horizon. I wanted to die while I was alive, but now that I was dying, I wanted to live.

Although I had more or less intellectually resigned myself to my death, physically, the body was resisting death. No, that's not right either. The body was praying for death, to be put out of its misery. It was some miniscule insignificant indefinable amoebic force inside which I might as well call the spirit, for lack of a better word, that wanted to survive. But I didn't at all feel spiritual either. It felt desperately, pathetically, mindlessly protozoan.

And I understood the disdain of my superior observer. I had betrayed my own original intent to take my life. This journey had been a suicide mission. And yet, at the last moment, I was pathetically showing my lack of resolve. After all, I had nothing to live for. So it was irrational for me to

3

want to live. And it was the rational realization of that irrational truth that compelled me to take the last step of my final act. But as I began to slip myself over the gunwale into the sea, I heard a voice.

"Excuse me."

2   IN-BETWEEN BROWS

```
    •        •

         •

      ——————
```

I turned and saw an emoticon sitting on the opposite gunwale.

"I have a book for you, which I wrote," he said.

Imagine that. What I expected to hear was something like, "How are you? Do you need help? What can I do for you?"

I was outraged by his failure to notice my plight. I wanted to scream, "What do I care about a stupid book? Can't you see I'm dying?" But my parched throat felt like cracked leather and no words issued forth.

"Free of charge," he offered. The book had a picture of a girl on the cover, with the name Les Dan Nil as author. It was, of course completely soaked and bloated with water.

It occurred to me then that he was probably insane, straining my own sense of sanity for interacting with him. He was lost at sea like I was, who knows for how long, and the excruciating experience had made him mad. Just my rotten luck,

I thought.

"It's about my Melody" he went on. "She liked lilies."

I was not moved.

"If you have a pen, I could sign it for you."

I tried to move closer to him to whisper some profanities, but my voice continued to fail me.

"I was on a book tour you see," he said. "I was one of the many featured authors on a cruise for book fans. High brows, low brows and in-between brows. It was a relatively small ship compared to the more modern, gargantuan 'floating city' super liners, but I was most grateful nevertheless to take part in such an occasion."

"So what?" I retorted silently in my mind. "I may be dying, but I'm still somebody, aren't I? Much more important than a stupid book." Although my sense of identity had vanished in my prolonged state of solitude, it seemed to be reasserting itself in the presence of another being.

"It's been a rewarding journey," he said. "When you're in the spotlight, you feel like you matter for the moment. But when the spotlight fades, the only thing that shines for you is who you love."

I had no idea who this Melody was but I hated her. Why should she, who was not present, deserve more consideration than I did? When Les handed me the book, I violently threw it overboard. That vicious burst of emotion drained me. I had no strength to plea my case for recognition and acknowledgment.

Looking dismayed, Les said, "How unfortunate." Then he remained silent for a long while. Finally he said, "I suppose I could give you an account of the story from memory."

"Not interested," would have been my reply if my throat hadn't felt like dried cracked desert soil. As Les continued to speak, he never mentioned even a single kind word to alleviate my condition. "What a heartless monster," I thought. "I'm not going to listen to you!"

But his voice was all there was in that great windless ocean. So I listened against my will. For my will could not defy his omnipresence. But I had to admit, my desperate need for recognition out in that vast empty space did find more than a small measure of relief and satisfaction in his appearance. Of course I wouldn't dare show any kind of gratitude to him. I wasn't there to make friends.

As he went on with his tale, I slowly learned about Melody and Emoticonda, the island nation where Les came from. It was part of a separate world almost exactly like ours, with nearly the same geography and history, in some parallel universe, but only inhabited by emoticons. Thus in their usage, the terms men and women, referred only to them, rather than human beings. In fact, I was probably the only human he had ever encountered. But I never got a chance to ask him.

3 FIRST-HAND VOICE

Apparently in Emoticonda, Les was as nondescript as an emoticon could be. He was the kind of emoticon you would not notice in a crowd of emoticons. Actually you might notice him because he looked so minimal. In his mind, he was a giant walking billboard of plainness in plain sight of the entire world.

It was a peculiar position to be in. On the one hand he felt anonymous and invisible because of his plainness. On the other hand he felt his anonymity and invisibility made him stand out like a pale white potato in a bowl of red tomatoes. It was like being a famous nobody or a totally unknown somebody. He could not even equate himself to a "has-been" because he had never been a "been" in the first place.

This is why it stressed him to go out in public. His nondescript presence only served to confirm his insignificance. Wherever he went, his painful plainness followed him like a relentless shadow. He felt as if he were his own stalker. Sometimes he wished his stalker deadly success so that he could be put out of his misery. But he was too much of a coward to carry out his own demise.

Likewise it stressed him to remain at home where his self-imposed solitude also confirmed his lack of identity. He was not only a nobody to others, he was a nobody to himself. Could anyone be a bigger failure than that? He wished desperately to disassociate himself from himself and become somebody else. But he didn't know how to become somebody else because he had always been only himself. He was stuck in a no-win situation.

He lived at Nameless Beach which had been bequeathed to him by his late grandfather, who had been an Olympic gold medalist. That feat had put the relatively unknown island of Emoticonda on the world map. Which in turn, resulted in a building boom by investors, and the flourishing tourist industry was set in place.

The island bestowed the Nameless Beach property to Les's grandfather as a token of gratitude. He made a personal pledge to maintain the beach in a pristine state, somewhat dismayed by the commercialization of the rest of the island beaches. And so the property had remained untouched.

Les also received a modest monthly sum from an annuity his grandfather had set up for him. Having virtually no expenses, Les put most of that amount back into his own savings. The beach was forbidden to the public as it was private property. The only other beach designated for private use on Emoticonda was Melancholy Beach. But at least it had the distinction of having a proper name.

The sandy strip of Nameless Beach was one mile long. The open area of the property extended for another half mile in width to the backdrop of the tropical forest, which was an additional mile wide. The entire area was surrounded by an outcropping of giant boulders that formed a protective semicircular barrier. Thus a few locals alluded to Nameless Beach as "Boulder Bowl."

In fact some who resented Les's good fortune, but not his peculiar existence, called him "That Lucky Blunderhead Of Boulder Bowl." Les learned this from the acquaintances of his bar-tender friend, One-Eyed Lax, who used to live with him.

But no derogatory name-calling by others could make Les feel as bad as he made himself feel. After all, the comments of others essentially came second-hand, whereas his own voice came first hand.

4 NAMELESS DAY

Les lived in a tree house. It began as a very simple structure with a deck and a hammock with mosquito netting. However with the help of his friend, One-Eyed Lax, he turned it into an elaborate three-level dwelling spanning several eucalyptus and palm trees. They constructed roofing with thatched reeds and layers of palm fronds. To maintain a feeling of openness, they only built three permanent walls, while the fourth was hinged at the ceiling and hoisted in the raised position with some ropes and pulleys, so that it could be lowered to shut out inclement weather. Two opposing walls were comprised of lattice works covered with honeysuckle vines. On each level there was a swing and a hammock as well as a shallow sand box covered by quilts and sheets which served as a bed. Sometimes he slept in the hammock, other times in the bed.

Les had a daily routine. He awoke at dawn to the sound of the forest songbirds and quickly rappelled down or took the ladder to the ground. Then he walked past the sea oats and morning glories towards the water. The seagulls took to the air at his approach and the sandpipers scurried out of his way. The beach faced east, the sun rising dead center. A barrier reef in the distance sheltered the waters from the wild outer waves. As the sun flushed the sea with its glittering light, he began his morning swim.

Afterward he went fishing from one of the furthermost boulders in the water. Once his catch of the day was in hand, he climbed back up the ladder to his open kitchen deck which protruded beyond the overhang of leaves. Within a circular stack of rounded stones, bedded by sand, he set his campfire aflame and pan-fried his breakfast with some garlic, onions and tomatoes. He accompanied that with fresh squeezed orange juice and a cup of hot fresh mint tea sweetened with honey.

It took the rest of the morning for him to go through his round of duties. First he checked the condition of the vegetable garden. Whatever he pared off the plants, he cast upon the compost pile.

Next he walked through the spacious orchard of indigenous and non-indigenous fruit trees, arriving at the far end of the beach where he had set beehive boxes.

At that point, he went up into the canopy to ride and check his zip line network that crisscrossed through the forest. It also took him up to the ridge of boulders where pools of rainwater cascaded down into an aqueduct system of split bamboo which led to the tree house to serve his drinking, washing and showering needs. One additional pool served as a hot tub, absorbing the heat of the tropical sun during the day.

By then it was well past noon. He had soup and salad or a sandwich for lunch, sitting at the picnic table on a wooden deck on the beach. After cleaning up, he took a siesta lying on the soft sand of the beach.

When he awoke, it would be late afternoon. He

would go snorkeling in the waters of the cove. If he felt like having fish again for dinner, he would bring along his spear gun. Then he barbecued the catch with a side dish of grilled vegetables on a skewer and baked yam.

By the time he finished washing up, it would be nightfall. He had no electricity on the premises. He used torches and candles for nightlight, though he did have flashlights for emergency use. He went to sleep looking out at the stars and listening to the gentle waves falling along the shore as the fragrance of honeysuckle and jasmine in the tropical breeze passed over him.

And that pretty much summed up his day—an insignificant one by an insignificant being at an insignificant place. Some might say Les lived an enviable care-free life of a beachcomber at a perfect hideaway. It was a virtual Garden of Eden. But no place was a sanctuary for someone who disliked himself. He arrived at the completion of the day without any true joy.

This uneventful existence of haunting anonymity took a turn for the worse when three dreams came to Les on three successive nights. They came without warning, simply out of the blue, or what his grandfather used to call "The Blue Sleep."

5   THE PRESSING SKY

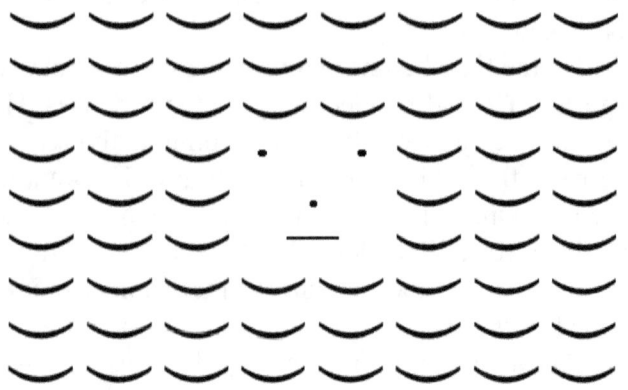

In the first dream, Les Dan Nil found himself at sea. He was treading water surrounded by a blank horizon under a blank sky, with nothing but blankness as far as he could see. The emptiness of the sky mirrored the emptiness of the sea.

Then with diabolical menace, the sky solidified into a massive transparent crystal. The base of that sky began to descend, inching its way toward Les. It made contact with his head and pressed him downward. He took one frantic breath before he was forced underwater.

As the solid sky drove him deeper, the sea itself began to gel. He felt as if his own desperately flailing limbs were churning the water, speeding up its coagulation. He realized this was his burial at sea. He was facing death without ever having been anyone of consequence. The painful heaviness of that knowledge was greater than the weight of the pressing sky.

Then the emerald sea solidified around his legs. It quickly encased his abdomen and chest. A moment later, his face and head were sealed, entrapping him like some ancient insect preserved in transparent blue amber.

In that instant, Les awoke in a panic, gasping for air. He fell out of his hammock onto the wooden floor. He felt as if his wildly pounding heart were in his throat choking him. He thought he might have to stop his heart in order to breathe. He scrambled to the rope and swung himself down to the beach. He fell when he landed, tumbling over the sand.

He looked back at his tree house by the predawn light. It had been his personal refuge, a sanctuary to which he could retire after a full day of activities. It was an altar from which he could lord over his private domain. But it no longer seemed welcoming. It looked ominous and threatening, as if it were a silent partner of The Blue Sleep. They were cohorts with malicious intent. They were set upon destroying him.

He turned and faced the sea. He wanted to run into the water and dive in to clear his mind of the dream. But the dream still left a deadly imprint on his mind, casting a threatening specter upon the innocent serenity of the sea before him. He stutter-stepped frantically back and forth, afraid to enter the water. Even the momentary sinking of his every step into the yielding sand reminded him of the dream's fatal curdling sea.

Frustrated by his own indecisiveness, he threw himself down on the sand. He looked up at the sky, daring it to turn to crystal. He gave it a moment. No, it was not solidifying. But there was something devious about that. In fact, the breathless beauty of the morning seemed an act of deceit by Mother Nature. How dare she make everything look so cheerful?

She didn't know anything about his troubles. She was totally oblivious to his plight. He was not going to stand for her luminous scenario. No. The dream had doomed him to a gloomy day and he wasn't going to have it any other way. He was determined to defy Mother Nature and have himself a dismal day.

And to insure the ruin of his day, he asked himself the same questions he had been asking himself forever. One: "Who am I?" And two: "What's wrong with me?"

There was no answer to the first question. There never was. As for the second question, there were a million answers. "You don't count. You don't add up to much. If you were a number you couldn't even be divided, much less subtracted because there's nothing to take away. You're a valueless number of absolute negative sum zero."

"You're a blank-face, a blank-head, a blankety blank wet blanket with not even a blank cover story to explain your blank identity!"

"You're what's left after every thing's been erased, a leftover erasure remnant, a walking erasure face, whose life is a completely preempted, whitewashed white-out!"

And that's how the rest of the day went, his own discouraging words berating him as he resumed his duties by rote.

That night at bedtime, he stood facing his hammock, dreading The Blue Sleep. The only way to avoid it was to remain awake. But sleep was the only thing that stopped him from having to listen to his debilitating self-talk. It was a trap. Sleep and you're doomed. Awake and you're doomed. He made several circuits around the tree house, going from level to level. Eventually, from sheer fatigue and exasperation, Les collapsed into the hammock and fell asleep .

6   SEEING BLIND

Right on cue, The Blue Sleep sent Les another devastating dream. This time he found himself freezing in a stark winter landscape. Actually he could not see much of the landscape due to the blinding blizzard. Driven by howling winds, the snow pelted him from all directions. There were no landmarks to give him any bearing--no trees, no hills, no mountain peaks. He stood amidst a flat field of snow within a small circle of visibility. Everything beyond that was a formless wall of white infinity. Seeing nothing to see, he might as well have been seeing blind.

Despite his winter clothing, his fingers and toes burned with pain from the unforgiving cold. The searing wind and snow were sandpapering his face. His exposed nose felt as if the wind chill had scraped off a layer of its skin. He wished he could cut off his nose to be rid of the pain. He folded his arms to get some feeling into his gloved hands. He stomped his feet to do the same for his toes.

Already the snow was shin deep where he stood. Though he had no idea where to go, he began to walk forward, grimacing against the snow stabbing his eyes.

Each step became an increasing struggle as the layer of snow rose at an alarming rate. It wasn't long before the snow was up to his knees. Then in no time it was thigh high. He was now inching ahead by dragging his feet because he could not lift them. Sooner than he realized, the snow surrounded his waist in a firm hold. By the time the accumulated snow tightened around his chest, Les could not move his feet at all. The snow was solidifying into ice.

He threw himself forward in an attempt to swim ahead with his arms. But the rest of his body was locked in place by the vise like grip of the glaciation, which now encased his neck. Frozen mucous filled his nostrils. He fought for air, breathing through his mouth, only to take in white powder choking him. Amidst his coughing fit, he could feel the chilling immobilization of his face.

It was a familiar scene from the dream of the night before. This time it was the body of snow, rather than the body of water, that was cementing his fate. Instead of blue amber, it was opaque ice. Deprived of breath, Les was overcome with desperate grief and sorrow.

He was suffering another unacknowledged death in a remote nameless place with no one to witness his passing. He had lived a life of anonymity and now he was going to die in anonymity, without even a tombstone or a wooden cross to signature his passage. There would be no mourning by anyone at this vast storming graveyard.

A sudden surge of anger rampaged through him. He raged against his ineptitude, his incompetence, his failure to fulfill anything of note. As his collapsing lungs struggled to burst free, he felt full of bitterness over his wasted life. It could not offer him any solace or deliverance. Aside from his burning anger, his body felt completely numb, as if his body itself were ice, as if it had already become inorganic, at one with the deadness of the lifeless cold.

But Les Dan Nil awoke in time again to escape from death.

It was dawn. Full of fear and fury, he stormed to the nearest wall and ripped off the honeysuckle vines. He rappelled down and ran to the beach, stomping on the morning glories on the way, then chased the sandpipers and screamed at the seagulls taking flight. He ran back up to his vegetable garden, shook the fencing and hopped about inside, crushing everything in sight as if he were on a trampoline. He knocked the first scarecrow down, then the second. He ran among the trees, punching the hanging fruit, like a crazed inept boxer.

When his rage was spent, he collapsed on the

sunlit sands and looked up at the serene blue sky of indifference.

He remained there until noon.

Then he arose and looked about the wasteland that he had created. He spent the rest of the day cleaning up after himself and restoring some semblance of order.

As he did so, he found a strange and absurd comfort in the familiarity of his cruel and invalidating monologue of the mind. That was more like his usual self. The self he knew. The one who had just gone on a rampage was an unfamiliar self. That self certainly gave him no comfort. He preferred the quietly suffering discouraged Les. That was his identity. It was the same old Les who constantly admonished himself by saying things like, "You're a numberless number, less than least, a major minor past none, all for naught, a missing link linking nothing, on permanent un-link."

"You're on disconnect, a discard entire of itself, unplugged, out of charge, out of luck, out of pluck—over and out, full of doubt, no way out."

But by nightfall, the comfort of his destructive diatribe became wearisome. Should he not simply throw the white flag at The Blue Sleep and die in his dream as his grandfather did? Perhaps it was in his genes. Maybe he came from a long line of dream-die-ers. Well, he was too fatigued to even entertain the idea of staying up all night to avoid The Blue Sleep.

What did he have to live for, really? Every day was the same as the next, so you couldn't tell one from the other. And you couldn't remember what you did from one day to the next because of the very sameness of the deeds. Besides, there was no point in remembering the days when it all came down to one day being lived the same way over and over. And without memory, what were you? A blank slate. Which is what he was. A blank being.

So with resignation, Les Dan Nil lay himself down to sleep, hoping The Blue Sleep would indeed fulfill its stealth purpose and deliver his death.

7 WINDY SALAD

The Blue Sleep did not disappoint him. It brought a third dream in which Les found himself alone in a landscape devoid of any features. In fact there was no landscape at all. Suddenly a fierce wind picked him up. Then it tossed him all about, as if he were a shred of lettuce in a windy salad. As far as he could tell, there were no other ingredients flying around with him in that chaotic anarchy of winds.

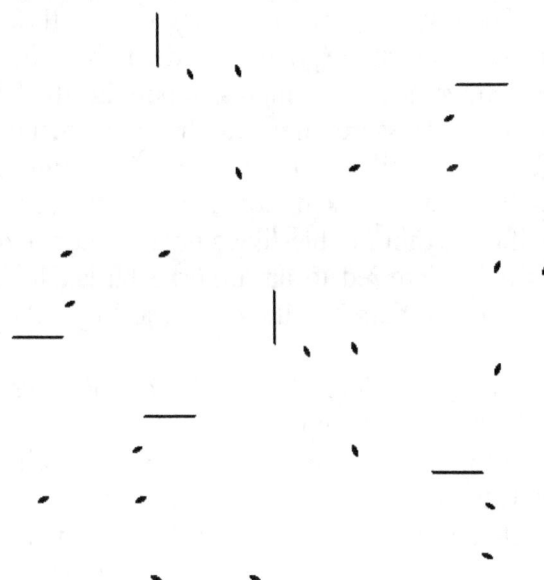

He remained airborne, without sight of ground, without sight of sky. It was an empty colorless space full of nothing but ferocious fury of the roaring winds. He had no idea which way was up or down. He was tumbling, rolling, spinning, cartwheeling; backwards, forwards, sideways, all at once. He was going nowhere at accelerating speed.

The gale force winds whipping him about were so strong he thought his limbs would be ripped apart. They crushed him against thrusting walls of other winds. Not only that, the winds were suffocating him, robbing him of breath by stuffing him with wind. He was drowning by the force-feeding of air.

Then with demonic malevolence, the winds changed their strategy. In a unified show of force, they converged to compress upon his body with enormous pressure, freezing his movements. The effect was similar to his two previous nightmares. His body was locked down and paralyzed, as if petrified within marble-like amber of the winds. He was being interred to an airborne burial, his lungs filled to its bursting limit. It was now the final moment.

And just before he lost his consciousness, Les awoke from the dream.

And he felt outrage at finding himself alive. The Blue Sleep had betrayed him. It had toyed with him, tempting him with death for two nights, then broke that promise on the third night. It was abominable. He felt himself the brunt of a malicious joke.

He was being victimized by The Blue Sleep

because he was just the kind of person that could be easily victimized. And the Blue Sleep knew it. If he were somebody else, The Blue Sleep would never send him nightmares. If he were somebody else, he could stand up to The Blue Sleep and none of this would be happening.

That was it in a nutshell. Everything that happened to him happened because he was who he was. If he wanted things to change, he had to change. If he wanted another life, he had to become somebody else. But being who he was prevented him from changing because, he was, in fact, a person who could not change. It was a double bind. He could not escape being himself.

He chose to internalize his anger, rather than venting it by acts of desecration he had carried out the day before. Additionally, and paradoxically, though full of wrath, he also felt emotionally squashed by the winds of the dream. He looked about his abode, then to the beach and the sea. He half expected the scenery to look squashed as well. It would have been a sympathetic sign that the world shared his woes.

But no, the world looked the same as usual. It remained stoic, uncaring of his plight. This further confirmed his pathetic outcast status.

Completely demoralized, Les could no longer deal with the effects of his nightmares alone. He had to get help. He was worn down from his solitary war of mind. He had to go see his friend, One-Eyed Lax at Happy Hour Beach.

8   YES SHOW

Les had first met One-Eyed years ago, before the tree house was completed and he was living in a tent. One morning, Les got up for his usual swim and saw One-Eyed's body lying on the sand. It looked like a corpse washed up by the sea. Les rushed over to find him still breathing, and reeking of alcohol.

When Les tried to awaken him, he mumbled, "Let me die. Just let me die."

Les did not see any outer wounds. So he shook One-Eyed again and asked, "Do you feel any internal injuries?"

One-Eyed raised himself up on one elbow and threw up. "There's my internal injury," he said and lay his head back down in the pool of vomit.

"Do you need a doctor?"

"Too late. A mortician."

"Should I call an ambulance?"

"A hearse is more up my alley."

"I can't help you if I don't know what's wrong."

"The only thing wrong with me is a jabbering idiot in my face who won't shut up."

"I'm just trying to find out . . ."

"Hey, buddy. Ease up, all right? Just let me die in peace."

"You can't die here," Les said in a panic.

"Last I heard, a man can die anywhere."

"But not here."

"Bet I can prove you wrong."

"I'm calling an ambulance. Don't move. I have to run to a payphone at the convenience store."

One-Eyed grabbed Les's arm. "You stay put. If you don't shut up, I'll kill you right here and now."

Les backed away. He took a second look at One-Eyed. Was this the face of a man who could commit murder? Les decided to give One-Eyed some space and left him alone for the rest of the day.

Around dinner time, One-Eyed finally roused himself up and calmly joined Les for a light meal. One-Eyed did not explain how or why he ended up at Nameless Beach and Les did not ask. The conversation was mostly one-sided, with One-Eyed asking the questions and Les giving the answers. When One-Eyed ran out of questions he asked to stay the night. Les let him take the hammock. That stay extended to a few more days. Then it expanded to a week, two weeks. Before Les knew it, six months had passed by.

During that time One-Eyed did help Les construct the three-story, split-level tree house, after his working hours tending bar. Once the tree house was completed, Les moved up and offered one of the other levels to One-Eyed. But he opted for the tent that Les had vacated. It was then that they began work on the extensive zip-line network. They also widened and smoothed out the footpath through the boulders that ran between the pineapple plantation and Nameless Beach.

As befit his bar-tender persona, One-Eyed brought home a party crowd to Nameless Beach once or twice a week. Much to Les's chagrin, he discovered he possessed a position of notoriety with some of One-Eyed's guests. They expressed surprise and honor at meeting him.

"So you're The Nameless Nobody of Nameless Beach! Let me shake your hand!" Or "At last, The Legendary Looney of Limbo-Land! I'm blown away!" And less abrasive but the most obscure, "My man! The Mad Hatter of Mad-hattan!"

Some of the girls were indeed intrigued by Les and his unique situation and warmed up to him, but he was not comfortable partaking in pointless liaisons that ended when the sun came up.

Curiously enough, One-Eyed did not participate directly in the parties. He remained on the fringe of the festivities, sometimes retreating to the tent to strum on a guitar which he had picked up through a friend of a friend. He was a virtual no-show at his own party. And by default, Les became the yes-show. It was a position Les craved to denounce.

Needless to say, the parties played havoc with Les's compulsively routine existence. The tree house was in constant state of disorder and disarray. The zip-lines too needed repairs as some of the guests, in a drunken state, would triple up or quadruple up on each other, straining the lines, causing a fall and injuries. Thus he spent most of the daylight hours cleaning up the aftermath of the previous night.

As his discontent and frustrations grew, at the sixth month point of One-Eyed's stay, Les was ready to ask him to leave. As it turned out, Les did not have to bring up the subject. One-Eyed left on his own, due to an unexpected twist of fate.

One-Eyed had composed a song called "Coyote Chow." He sang it regularly at the bars on Happy Hour Beach. One day an agent, who was on holiday, heard One-Eyed and signed him up on the spot. That was the day One-Eyed moved out of Nameless Beach. Eventually, the song became a world-wide hit and One-Eyed earned a fortune. With that he bought Happy Hour Beach, also known as The Double-H, and leased out its twenty five bars. That was a long time ago, but One-Eyed still stayed in touch, coming by once in a blue moon to fish with him, or ride the zip-lines. He always came alone, respecting Les's need for solitude.

9 BARKING UP

Happy Hour Beach was actually a small circular island. The mastermind behind its concept was a former celebrity cowboy film star, now deceased, who had always dreamed of retiring at a lush tropical island to forget his dry desert origins. It was just large enough for twenty four bars built right next to each other in a circular configuration. From the air, it looked like a giant twenty-four hour clock.

Each bar had its own distinctive look and decor. And each bar offered happy hour for one hour, at which time the next bar took over. After the Midnight Bar had its happy hour, the Shoot For The Moon Bar had its happy hour, followed by the Splash Down Bar, then Walk On Fire Bar, and so on. In the center of that clock face, there was a twenty-fifth bar, called the Hall Of Fame Bar, attended by sports celebrities, visiting film stars, and other VIP's.

There was no docking or anchoring of boats permitted at Happy Hour Beach. Even jet skis were forbidden. That was to prevent drunk driving. Thus the only way to access Happy Hour Beach was by the transparent undersea tunnel called Wonder Mile Walkway. The two outer lanes were designated for pedestrians. The two inner lanes were for the two-way traffic of electric golf carts. Some served as taxis and others served as delivery vehicles. The speed limit was set at ten miles an hour.

After getting off the bus at the entrance to Wonder Mile Walkway, Les hurried through the underwater tunnel. Considering his recent drowning dream, he was in no mood to linger along the length of the submerged seascape to marvel at its beauty. It was too reminiscent of his forced submersion by the crystal sky. He had a moment of panic, imagining the tunnel suddenly caving in to fulfill the drowning he had barely escaped in his dream. Perhaps the dream was a premonition of his death here and now! He sighed in relief when he finally made it through to the firm sands of Happy Hour Beach.

It was only nine o'clock in the morning, but sure enough, the Bottoms Up Bar was packed with college-age tourists intent on completing the infamous Happy Hour Beach 24-Hour Grand Prix. The Grand Prize was a two-week all-expenses-paid holiday for two at an all-inclusive five-star resort of choice plus $10,000 cash and a Free Lifetime Pass to the VIP Bar. Needless to say, no one had ever come close to winning the prize, except for the local magnate, Sir Wintry Cubeheart. He was the only man to triumph over the circuit but he could not claim the prize because the competition was only officially open to tourists. However, he did make good use of his Free Pass to the VIP bar to hobnob with the rich and famous to eventually finance the building of his brainchild, the Blossom Ice Palace.

Luckily, One-Eyed had finished his shift at the Rub Your Eyes Bar and was now lying in a hammock suspended from palm trees near the water's edge. Although he was the owner of the entire domain, he occasionally pulled a shift bar tending to keep his form. It was his way of remaining humble despite his wealth. In fact, he did not own a home. He lived on Happy Hour Beach like a true beachcomber, sleeping in the hammocks or the reclining beach chairs, or sometimes just directly on the sand. And much to the chagrin of his agent, he never wrote another song.

"Long time no see," One-Eyed said, sitting up.

"Have you ever died in your dream?" Les asked.

"What?"

"My grandfather once told me that if you die in your dream, you die in real life."

"If I did die in a dream, I wouldn't live to tell you about it."

"That proves my point."

"What point?"

"I'm going to die."

"An aye to that. We all are."

"But I can't die in a dream."

"I don't think you get to choose."

"No. I mean I can't die as me. I have to die as somebody else."

One-Eyed Lax sat up in his hammock and took a good hard look at Les Dan Nil. "Now listen up. I've known you for quite a spell now, and this is about the most cockamayme thing I ever heard. How do you reckon to pull off this crazy idea?"

"I don't know but I've got to change."

"So you can die?"

"Yes, because I can't stand to be me anymore."

"What's wrong with being you?"

"You name it."

"Everybody's got something wrong with 'em."

"With me it's everything."

"Supposing you could be somebody else. Who would you be?"

"That's the other problem. I don't know. I've never been somebody else, so I don't know who to be."

"Then you're right back where you started."

"Tell me about it."

"I just did."

"This is no laughing matter."

"What in Hades do you think I can do about all this?"

"You know people. You're a bartender. You've met thousands of people. You listened to their troubles. They told you their secrets. You know how they got to be who they are. You know what makes them tick and un-tick."

"And you got some un-ticking to do."

"This is serious. You've got to help me."

One-Eyed Lax looked out to sea, past the tourists lying on the sand. Some sat in their beach chairs sipping their drinks. Others were wading in the water taking snapshots. A few were floating on their air mattresses as swimmers passed them by. One-Eyed sighed and said, "I never did tell you how I lost my other eye, have I?"

"No. I never asked out of politeness."

"Well, it's that time now. 'Cause it may show you, you're barking up the wrong tree."

10 BARKING DOWN

"There was a girl," One-Eyed said wistfully . . .

Her name was Serena. She came to me at sunrise, here on this beach. Right there, right out of the water, all wet in a white dress. She was like some ocean angel. Talk about a sunrise surprise. I had a hangover and a half but that cleared up in a flash when I saw her. I thought I was dreaming. She didn't see me at first. She was looking at a seashell in her hand. Anyway when she got up on shore, I said a mouthful of words. To this day, I don't know what I said. She was so damned beautiful I couldn't think straight. My mind was all jumbled up.

"What did you say?" she asked.

"Haven't a clue," I said. "I'm like that first thing in the morning. I wake up jabbering about

nothing. It wasn't anything mean, though. I'm sure of that."

"You don't look the mean type," she said.

"Oh, but you. I can see a mean streak in you, all right."

She smiled and asked, "Is this normal?"

"What?"

"All these people sleeping on the beach."

"What do you expect from drunken tourists?"

"So you're a tourist too?"

"I was. Originally, a long time ago."

"Lucky you."

"It wasn't luck. It was a decision."

"That's all my friends have talked about ever since setting foot on this place – moving here to live. That's them sleeping in those hammocks there."

"You should follow their lead."

"They'd never really actually make the move. They just like to hear themselves talk. Still, I have to admit, it's a beautiful island. I'd love to stay forever. But I have a life at home. It would take something totally extraordinary to get me to live here for good."

"It's gotta be love then."

"What do you mean?"

"The thing that's gonna get you to stay."

"Love's not that big a deal. Everybody's always falling in love. Then out of love. Happens every day. Nothing extraordinary about it."

"So you've had experience?"

"Oh, you know. So far, just dating kind of stuff, I guess."

"We could work on it."
"What?"
"On making something extraordinary."
"Dream on. I don't even know you . . ."

"And you know what? After two weeks, her friends went back home. But Serena stayed to be with me. It was a damned miracle. That's another story in itself. I still have that seashell she gave me. The one she found that morning."

Then One-Eyed looked away to the sea for a while, before continuing his commentary.

"She was something, that girl. Not a mean bone in her body. There were times when I'd look at her and wonder what the heck she was doing with me. She was too good for me. I just knew she was going to leave me someday for somebody better. Because I sure wasn't good enough for her. So, stupid me, I kept a roving eye out for other girls. They'd be my insurance for the day Serena left me. They'd cushion my fall when she dropped me."

"I think I know where this is going," Les said.

"Well, sure as hell under high water, Serena found out about my philandering, and she did leave me. And you know what? Those other girls didn't cushion my fall at all. I was so torn up inside and mad at myself, I gouged out my 'roving eye.' As soon as I got out of the hospital, I went on a tear with the bottles. And ended up at your place a few days later. Don't ask me how."

"I'm sorry about her. But what does that have to do with this tree I'm supposedly barking up?"

"The point is, the only time I ever felt like

somebody, was with Serena. And that stuff with the flock of tourist girls, I was never anybody to them. When their vacation was over, they just hopped back on their plane or cruise ship. You want to be somebody? Find yourself a Serena."

"That's not going to work for me. I'm a nobody. Nobody wants a nobody."

"I was a nobody until Serena came along."

"No. You have it backwards. I have to be somebody before somebody wants me."

"Now you're barking upside down that tree, you are."

"Forget your tree. I don't want anybody to want me anyway. All I want is to die. But I don't want to waste my dying on me."

"Well," One-Eyed sighed. "Your bark's got me stumped. Let me put my thinkin' cap on." After a short while he said, "You know what? There just might be a fella that could help you out. And I reckon that's my old compadre, Sir Wintry Cubeheart."

"The owner of the Blossom Ice Palace?"

"By his own words, he's been a dandy, a doorman, a dentist, a draftsman, a dean and a dunce; a deadweight, a duke and a drunk; not to mention a detective, a designated hitter and a double agent."

"Did you say 'duke?'"

"He was. Don't know how he got downgraded. But anyway, he's been everywhere, done everything. If anybody knows how to be somebody, it's gotta be him."

"Perfect."

"He doesn't come around here much anymore.

But we're still pretty tight amigos. He gave me a lifetime carte blanche to his park. We'll drop in on him."

11 COYOTES OF CHANCE

During their bus ride to Blossom Beach, One-Eyed had an addendum to his Serena story.

"The thing I got out of that whole mess, the thing I figured out, is that love and fear go hand in hand. It's a package deal. The second you fall in love, you're right smack dab in the middle of a losing proposition. The odds are fifty-fifty you're going to lose that person you love. In a flip of the coin you can get your heart ripped to shreds by the coyotes of chance. That's a pretty mean pack of fear staring at you in the face. And I dealt with that fear in the worst way possible. Instead of looking that fear straight in the eyes, I looked away . . . to other girls. And I got torn to pieces. I was mincemeat. Coyote chow."

"So that's who your song was about."

"Bless her heart. She ended up marrying some tourist guy who owned a yacht with a helicopter. Rumor was he was the head of some principality. A better man than me, I'm sure. Anyway, she deserves the best."

When they arrived at the massive, domed amusement park, One-Eyed showed his lifetime Platinum Blossom Card. They were ushered in by a special attendant, past the tourists waiting in line. Inside, the Ice Palace was like a Christmas wonderland. Through the machine-generated snowfall, you could see sparkling lights adorning the pine trees, the various rides, the concession stands and the cafes and restaurants.

Despite the bright and cheerful ambiance, Les could not help but feel uneasy that the snowy setting was eerily reminiscent of his second deadly dream. He felt some dark force compelling him forward to this moment, to this place, even though the shadows were cast in white.

They were taken up in a glass elevator to the top floor, then into Sir Wintry's enormous office with floor-to-ceiling windows which provided a 360 degree overview of the park.

He was wearing a pair of unusual looking sunglasses which made him look like a friendly rogue bandit.

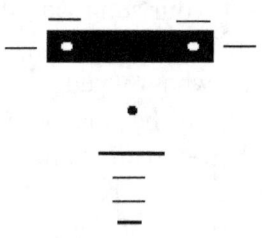

After initial pleasantries, Sir Wintry offered each of them a pair of sunglasses similar to his own. "I suffer from a rare and chronic form of snow-blindness so I'm required to wear these at all times. Every visitor to my park is offered one as a memento."

By-passing further chit-chat, One-Eyed said to Sir Wintry, "Believe it or not, we're here because Les wants to be somebody."

"Well, I've been a dandy, a doorman, a dean and a . . ."

" . . . dunce," Les blurted out. It was quite out of his character to be so brazen but he was in a desperate state, and did not want to waste any time.

Sir Wintry took no offense and gave a chuckle. "I'm flattered my renown precedes me to such a great extent," and rubbed his chin thoughtfully. He showed great restraint and patience for someone of his stature, or perhaps because of his stature.

"Have you ever died in a dream?" Les asked.

With a sly grin of amusement, Sir Wintry replied "No, not that I can recall."

"That proves my point," Les said.

"And what point may that be?" Sir Wintry asked.

"I'm going to die in my dream."

"I don't follow."

"He's got it in his head that his grandfather died in his dream," One-Eyed explained.

"That's impossible to know, isn't it?" Sir Wintry smiled.

"A man believes what a man believes."

One-Eyed shrugged his shoulders. "Proof don't matter none."

"Call me crazy," Les said. "But that's beside the point. I just have to be somebody before I die."

"Aren't you somebody now?"

"Now who's crazy? Please don't insult me. Look at me. I'm obviously a nobody. That's why we're here. With your collection of identities, we thought you could show me how to be somebody."

"I appreciate being held in such high esteem. But despite having been an adventurer extraordinaire, as some have claimed, I humbly submit, there was only one time in my life that I truly felt that I was someone."

Les felt an uneasy foreboding at the familiarity of that statement.

"Do you know why this place is called the Blossom Ice Palace?"

"Please don't let it be another girl-story," Les prayed in silence.

12   ARCTIC AWAKENING

Sir Wintry asked his staff for some privacy. After they left the room, he began his story.

Not too many people know what I'm about to tell you. I don't mention it too often, because it pains me to recount the grievous tale. I prefer to keep the event to myself, but your plea seems so earnest, and the fact that you are One-Eyed's friend, I'm moved to make an exception in your case. As you may know or not, once upon a time, I had the good fortune to be made a duke by the King of Emoticonstein, for saving the life of his queen. The details of that story can wait for a more appropriate occasion.

So there I was, living in a castle in my very own duchy, with the wealth and respect and prestige that comes with it. But something was missing. There's nothing like the enormity of a castle to make you realize the emptiness of your solitary existence. I felt a great lack despite my worldly possessions amidst the parade of guests and servants. I became melancholy.

I felt like a cast off seed or bulb left forgotten in a dark cellar that was slowly decaying, decomposing. I yearned for the light to spur my breakthrough in order to flourish in a bright new world. Then one day, Blossom came into my life. That story too can wait for another time. But in that magical moment of our meeting, I knew in an instant, that she was the radiant element that I so craved. I was mesmerized and awakened to a new life by the touch of her singular, unusual, almost iconoclastic and whimsical beauty. I was rapturously smitten. I was the lord of the manor but a helpless captive gladly chained to her heart.

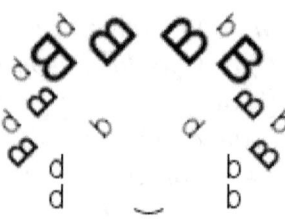

We were married within a fortnight. The happy occasion took place at sunrise at the duchy's lakeside. The wedding party of 300 guests in 30 hot air balloons were heading to the reception at the King's Palace a half an hour's flight away on the opposite shore.

During our ascent, a sudden gust sent our balloon crashing into another balloon above us, ripping the envelope. We plummeted into the lake and the impact knocked me unconscious. I regained consciousness a week later in the hospital at intensive care, my bones shattered. I found out everyone in our balloon had survived, despite injuries, except for Blossom, my bride.

I raged at the cruelty of fate to take such an innocent and gracious wonder as Blossom, still in the prime of her youth. Of all the souls in the world, she was the least that deserved to die. I myself no longer wanted to live. I tried to take my life, but after my first attempt the doctors kept me under 24-hour watch to prevent that outcome.

Eventually, I was cleared and released. Though my bones were mended, I was still a broken man inside. When I returned home, my castle felt like a hollow mausoleum. I forfeited my claim to the duchy and gave up my title as duke, to go into self exile. The King and Queen tried in vain to persuade me to stay. When they realized my decision was final, the King insisted on at least honoring me with knighthood as a farewell gift. I reluctantly relented even though a title added to my identity meant nothing to me. I felt I no longer had an identity. And so I took my departure.

I banished myself to the unforgiving regions of the Arctic. I thought I could numb the pain in my heart in the world of snow and ice. I lost all my toes and the first two joints of my fingers through frostbite from that time. Eventually, I realized, my heartache would never go away. The only way to kill the pain was to kill my love for Blossom. And I knew I could never do that. So finally, I understood, to keep the love alive, I would also have to keep the suffering alive. Otherwise, who am I without her?

Once I accepted my pain, I was able to start anew. That's when I came to this island, to bathe my pain in the sunlight. As luck would have it, I was able to build this kingdom of snow and ice to honor the memory of my long lost bride, the great love of my life, Blossom.

13   THE LONG REMAIN

When Sir Wintry finished speaking, a great and heavy silence weighed upon the room.

"So it was another girl-story," Les thought to himself. However, he was moved enough to show Sir Wintry proper respect. "I'm thankful for your sharing with me, a new-found stranger, your painful loss."

"I have been many things over the years. But the only time I truly felt my personage had any significance was with my beautiful Blossom."

"With all due respect," Les said. "There can be no Blossom for me as long as I remain the way I am."

"Of course you feel unworthy," Sir Wintry responded. "Do you think I ever thought I deserved Blossom? Not in the least. But that was what made her love for me so precious and miraculous."

"But I can't wait for a miracle to chance upon me. Death is knocking at the door of my dreams."

"Who knows how long your wait remains? A miracle can appear at any moment. I have given you the outpouring of my heart to offer the only answer I can to your plight."

"Believe me, I'm not ungrateful. But the answer you found for yourself is not the one for me. There must be another answer for me and I have to find it."

"You seek significance. And you shall have it when you give your all to another. Otherwise you remain undone."

"Well, nevertheless thanks again for your time, Sir Wintry."

"May I ask what your next step is?"

"Facing a dead end, as usual," Les replied.

"I see. I regret I was not able to help you. However there is one person who may provide the answer you seek. Do you know of Professor Prequel E. Sequel?"

"The crazy crackpot baker?"

"Perhaps. Perhaps not." Sir Wintry looked about the room. "What I'm about to tell you is quite hush hush."

Les and One-Eyed leaned forward in their chairs, toward Sir Wintry.

"This information was provided to me under the strictest confidence. And I trust the two of you will not betray that confidence which I am now requesting on your part."

"Sure thing, Cubeheart," One-Eyed said.

"Yes, of course," Les confirmed.

"Apparently the Professor is working on a special elixir. His theory is that ten thousand years from now, or a hundred thousand years from now, an emoticon will be a superior creature who has risen above the ills we still suffer today. Characteristics that incite such destructive behavior as deception, rage, violence, thievery, murder, warmongering will no longer exist in the heart and mind of a future emoticon. But rather than relying on the snail-pace process of evolution to take us to that transcendent state, he wants to create a means of leapfrogging that process instantaneously."

"So you end up with some kind of a super duper emoticon," suggested One-Eyed.

"Perfect!" exclaimed Les. "That's it. A Super Emoticon! That's what I want to be!"

"Please calm yourself," Sir Wintry said.

"And how's he planning to go about this business?" One-Eyed asked.

"I don't know much more than what I've told you."

"How do we get a hold of it?" Les asked.

"Not so fast, my friend," Sir Wintry said. "We must go about this discreetly. I am merely presenting a possibility."

"What's it going to take to see the Professor?"

"I don't know him personally," Sir Wintry said. "And he is a recluse. Never goes out in public. So we will need an intermediary to introduce us to him. Fortunately I've developed a friendship with the Professor's sales manager, Tip Top Burrows. He personally makes deliveries of the bakery goods to the Ice Palace. Indeed, I'm the bakery's biggest client."

"When can we meet Mr. Burrows?"

"He only works mornings and spends his afternoons at Hurricane Beach. We can visit him there to see if he'd be willing to introduce you to the Professor. In fact, I'm anxious to meet the Professor myself. He's such a mystery figure, I'd just like to satisfy my curiosity about him."

Then Sir Wintry gave Les two complimentary all-day passes to the Blossom Ice Palace.

"I doubt I will ever have the chance to use these," Les said.

"Take them nevertheless," Sir Wintry urged. "The future can surprise us in ways we cannot imagine."

14   BETWEEN ME

They drove down the Coastal Highway in Sir Wintry's snow-white stretch limousine until they arrived at Hurricane Beach Kite And Archery Club. The site was aptly named for its fierce and turbulent winds which roared through the inland canyons, and out to sea through a corridor formed by two massive cliffs facing each other.

When Les stepped out of the limo, he was instantly buffeted against the door by the gusting winds. He recalled his third dream and felt a chill run down the back of his neck. He once again imagined some dark power forcing him to arrive at this juncture in his fate. He gritted his teeth and followed the others holding onto a railing along a walkway that led to the Club House.

Once inside, they by-passed the indoor archery range and stepped out to a large veranda. They had an expansive view of the beach below. Half the beach was designated for use by stunt kite fliers and the other half for advanced archers.

A crowd of spectators on bleachers had their eyes on an archer wearing a quiver packed with arrows. About fifty yards beyond him on the beach stood a stunt kite flier. He wore a mask and an armor-plated suit, with his back to the audience. He leaned away from the open sea, holding his kite in the air at twelve o'clock position.

When a buzzer sounded from the observation tower, the stunt kite operator went into action, maneuvering his kite through high-speed acrobatics. In the meantime the archer shot arrow after arrow at breakneck speed. One of them pierced the kite, sending it crashing to the sand. A buzzer sounded twice from the tower. A point was awarded to the archer and the spectators gave applause.

During the brief pause the archer took another fully stocked quiver and threw it over his shoulder. The kite flier positioned another kite in the air. The buzzer sounded again and the action resumed. The sequence was repeated several times, with the archer downing more kites than not. The competition ended with the score 8 – 2 in favor of the archer. The spectators gave a rousing cheer.

When the archer entered the Club House, Sir Wintry approached him and made introductions. This was Tip Top Burrows. They went into the lounge and sat at a table.

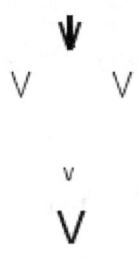

"I see you're looking at my tattoo," Tip Top said to Les, referring to the arrowhead marking on his forehead.

Les apologized and said, "Yes, I, ah, was looking at the workmanship . . ."

"It's a personal reminder," Tip Top said, smiling. "Not to repeat a regrettable mistake I made once. But no need to get into that now. What brings you here?"

"Our ambitious young man here, Les, wants to be somebody," Sir Wintry said.

"An honorable quest," Tip Top said.

"Have you ever died in a dream?" Les Dan asked.

"An interesting question. I can't be a hundred percent sure, but I'm inclined to say no."

"That proves my point," Les said, bitterly. "I'm going to die."

"We all are," everyone said in unison.

"I mean I'm going to die as me. I can't have that. The Blue Sleep has already made three attempts on my life. And I can't take a chance on its succeeding tonight."

"The Blue Sleep?"

"Never mind. Long story. The point is I have to die as somebody else."

"Would it be so tragic to die as yourself?" Tip Top asked.

"Maybe not for you. You're not a nobody."

"I appreciate the compliment, but if you're referring to my acquired skills as an archer, they mean little in the great scheme of things."

"But at least you have an identity. Even if it's only between you and you. There's none between me and me."

"Who is between you?"

"Nobody that counts."

"Because you're doing the counting."

"Okay, you count then. How many of me are there?"

"One. And isn't that enough?"

"It's zero from where I stand."

"Quite the conundrum, you see?" Sir Wintry said.

"Bull's eye," commented Tip Top. Then after a moment of silence, he continued. "Let me get this on the straight and narrow. You want to die with another identity, in order to avoid dying with your present identity?"

"Present non-identity," Les corrected him.

"But if you achieve another identity, there would be no need to die, since the previous non-identity would in fact, ipso facto, be dead."

"Oh," Les replied, suddenly dumbfounded. He had not expected this. He had to think it through.

Tip Top continued. "You say you want to die, but in truth, you want to live."

"That's brilliant," Sir Wintry said. "I have always admired your keen sense of observation."

"Nothing remarkable about it. You see, in order to shoot down a flying kite with my arrow, I cannot think as an archer, from the vantage point of my arrow. I must reverse my vision and see the kite from the kite's point of view. I must be the kite."

Continuing his own line of thought, Les said to no one in particular, "But if I go on living, I'll have to put up with so much stuff. I mean, living requires responsibilities."

"So says the current you," Tip Top replied. "But the new you, who would not be you at all, may not have these considerations. He may in fact, embrace life, and be invigorated by its challenges."

"Isn't there an easier way out?" Les asked

"That's still the now-you talking," Tip Top said.

"What a mess," Les said. "I thought I had everything figured out."

"What is your next step now?" Tip Top asked.

"Well," Les sighed. "You just threw a conundrum into my quandary. I know this is the now-me talking, but I can't talk as anybody else so I still say I don't want to be me. Alive or dead."

"And how do you plan to make that change?" Tip Top asked.

"You're the plan," Sir Wintry answered Tip Top.

"Me? I don't understand."

"Not exactly you, but you know someone who has a plan that might suit Les's plan."

Tip Top was quiet for a moment, a look of bewilderment on his face. And then he raised his eyebrows and lowered his voice to a whisper. "Of course. You mean the Professor, and his Evolution Accelerator Solution."

"Could you arrange a meeting with him for Les's sake?" Sir Wintry asked.

"Before we go down that dangerous road, let me tell you a story."

"I bet it's about a girl," Les mumbled to himself.

15   SOUND OF AIM

And so Tip Top began his tale:

Once upon a time in the days of my youth, I worked as an archer with a small traveling circus in Europe. My partner and companion was the great and only love of my life, Angela. The story of how we met and became the highest paid, most popular performers, and earned a fortune, can be saved for another time.

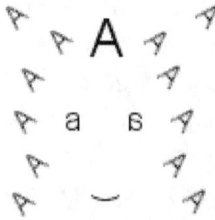

For now I will speak of Angela's ultimate dream, which was to have as many children as possible. Ten at least, twelve perhaps, even fourteen or sixteen. She wanted a household overflowing with love, she said. Considering we had both been runaway orphans at one time in our lives, her driving desire to fulfill such a dream was one I fervently shared.

To realize this dream, we pooled our savings and bought a piece of barren property here on this idyllic island of Emoticonda. And every year onward, we used our earnings to build, little by little, a homestead we named Eden Estate. Upon completion, our home comprised of sixteen bedrooms with an additional wing to serve as quarters for our servants and support staff.

The grounds had been designed to be a paradise playground for our future children. It contained an Olympic size swimming pool, three tennis courts - one hard, another clay and third grass, a baseball diamond, a beach volleyball court, a soccer field, a lake for water sports, a stable with five horses, a number of ducks, chickens, cats and dogs, pigs and sheep, and an indoor gymnasium with a basketball court, with a bowling alley annex.

After ten long years, we came upon our much anticipated final performance day. As usual we ended our act with our most dangerous phase. I first shot an arrow into an apple held in the palm of Angela's outstretched left hand. Then in her right hand. Followed by an apple set upon each shoulder. And as a coup de grace, I shot an arrow through an apple set on top of her head. But we were not done yet. For the grand finale, Angela was set on a spinning wheel with her arms and legs outstretched, similar to the famous drawing by Da Vinci. Once again, an apple was set in each hand, in holders above each shoulder, and the last above her head. And as the wheel turned, I shot my arrows into their mark.

Naturally, as usual we were rewarded with a resounding standing ovation. Knowing that this was our last performance for all time, the audience clamored for an immediate encore. Our contract only required one performance per day, unlike certain other acts which performed two or three times a day. But considering it was our final time, the owner begged to satisfy the spectators with an encore. He even offered a special bonus as a farewell gift. So after a half an hour of non-stop cheering by the crowd, we finally relented, but to repeat only the final spinning wheel phase for the encore.

By then the support crew, knowing the wheel was no longer of any use, had begun to destroy it. When the encore was announced, the crew hastily put the wheel back together, despite the damages. My trick to striking the target on the turning wheel was to count the sound of clicks the gears made. At the crucial moment, when I was aiming for the apple above Angela's left shoulder, a gear slipped, making me miscount, and my arrow shot straight into Angela's heart, killing her instantly.

16 NO ONE WANTS NO ONE

A great silence fell upon the room.

Tip Top wiped the tears from his eyes and looked out the window. "She was only twenty six. We had so many child-bearing years to look forward to."

Then he gave a heavy sigh. "In that moment of her death, I stuck an arrow into my head, intending to join Angela in her death. Eventually the arrow was removed by surgery. However I had a tattoo placed there to remind me of that great tragic day."

"And the Eden Estate?" One-Eyed asked.

" I awarded it to an orphanage which renamed it Angela's Home For Children. In the beginning I did volunteer work there, but it was too painful. So after several years of therapy, I took up archery again as part of the healing process."

"I'm sorry for your loss," Les said. "And I understand your point. The only time you truly felt like someone was with Angela. But that doesn't help me. I don't have an Angela."

Then he looked at Sir Wintry. "Or a Blossom."

Finally he eyed One-Eyed. "Or a Serena."

Then he gave a collective look at all of them. "Why do you think I'm still alone? Because nobody wants to be with a nobody like me. And the truth is, I don't want to be with anyone."

"I think the Professor is the last resort," Sir Wintry said.

Tip Top took a long quiet look at Les. "You

know there are tremendous risks involved with the Evolution Accelerator Solution."

"I'll take the chance. I'm nothing to lose," Les Dan Nil repeated.

After another moment of prolonged silence, everyone looked at each other, nodded in agreement and got up.

Tip Top went ahead in his car as the rest followed in the Blossom Limousine. During the drive, Les imagined what he might be like once he took the Evolution Accelerator Solution. As a highly evolved form of emoticon, he would truly be unique. He would stand out in a superior way. He would be taller, stronger, faster in his body, and brilliant in his mind. His thought processes would be ten times or even a hundred times faster than those of the average emoticon.

His emotional state would be rock solid. He would no longer suffer from any kind of debilitating, self-defeating self-talk. He would be able to rise above any turmoil and remain balanced and at peace. He might speak ten different language with ease as if they were his native tongue. He would be a phenomenal person.

People from all over the world would come to him with their problems and no matter how monumental they were, he would be able to find the solution with his advanced intellect. He could easily become the president of Emoticonda or the president of UN. He would solve the world's hunger problem, the jobless problem, the energy problem, the crime problem, the warmongering problem. The world would become a perfect place under his guidance. He would be the world's first and foremost super-emoticon ruler.

He was so excited with anticipation, lost in his revelry, that time flew by for him. And they arrived at the Professor's bakery-laboratory at Equation Beach before Les knew it.

Equation Beach was a horse-shoe shaped peninsula, twin protrusions out to sea that protected a tranquil cove. The Professor's place was set on a promontory at the inside curve of the horse-shoe. As they pulled up to the rear entrance of the building where the delivery trucks docked, Les was imagining himself going to sleep that night and waking up in the morning as Super-Les.

But wait, wasn't that a lot of responsibility? The ruler of the entire world? Maybe he should scale it down to being the president of Emoticonda. Or perhaps just the mayor of Emoticona. He could handle that, couldn't he? Well, he could always fall back on being the lord of Nameless Beach.

Les realized he was already filling himself with self-doubt. A typical thought pattern for him. It was infuriating. Even in his own day dream, in his own imagination, he was a loser in the end. How hapless and hopeless. And it was doubly frustrating to know exactly what the mind was doing yet remain unable to change it. That's why he had to pin all his hopes on that Evolution Accelerator Solution.

17 FRACTURED FRACTION

As they pulled up to the back of the building, Tip Top said, "Let me go ahead alone to make sure the Professor's agreeable to a meeting."

There were several delivery vans parked in a row at the loading dock. The words, "Medley Muffin Company" was painted on the side of each of them. They were all wet from having been washed and one of them was being wiped dry by a middle-aged uniformed worker.

q   p

"

When Tip Top got out of the limo, he said, "Looking good, Pedro."

The uniformed worker smiled and waved. Then he went back to wiping down the van.

About ten minutes later, Tip Top reappeared and motioned to the others to come in. The large bakery kitchen was all sparkling stainless steel and glowing white tile. They went into a small office where they were introduced to the Professor.

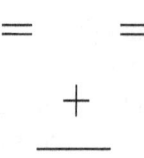

His assistant Stu Harking, who was paralyzed from the waist down, sat in an electric power chair. He looked as if he had gone through more than he had bargained for in life.

After the initial cordial chit-chat Tip Top explained to the Professor, "Les wants to be somebody."

Then Les gave a brief accounting of the Blue Sleep and his three dreams.

The Professor burst out, "Ah-ha, ha-ha.

Another fractured fraction. Are we all?"

Les was not sure what that meant but he was sure he didn't like it.

Then the Professor asked, "Do you have a venting fervent fever?"

"No," replied Les.

"Are you amiss with amnesia?"

"No."

"Taken a misstep with a Miss?"

"No, there is no Miss at all." Les was starting to get impatient with the Professor's non-pertinent questions.

"Musing melancholy for amnesty from murmurs of the heart?"

"What is all this mumbo-jumbo?" Les retorted. "I'm here because I don't want to be me anymore. If I'm somebody else, all my problems will go away."

"Ah-ha, ha-ha. Forget it. Render your surrender to the Big Number."

"What Big Number?" Les asked.

"The Biggest. Even as a fragile fractured fraction, minuscule as a follicle fool calibrating for leverage to an exponential entity, the yo-yo loop through the hoop is useless as a braille backhand."

"You're calling me a yo-yo?"

"No matter," replied the Professor. "Any lopsided anomaly is nominally anonymous, nearly null and innocuous as a nebula of navel lint . . ."

"I'm navel lint?" Les inquired incredulously.

" . . . until qualified to a potential sum by fusing to its convergent courting current," the Professor concluded.

"Keep in mind," Stu added. "Only that which

has value can be converted to another currency."

"So I'm like a country without currency?"

"No matter," continued the Professor. "Cash in on the burning bunch of yearning. Then you'll banish The Blue Sleep for Sunny Slumbers in less than a pinch of inch-time or a flatulence hiccup."

"I don't get it," Les protested.

"The Blue Sleep fumes are flaming forth from the infernal combustion of your toxic solitary hues. Melancholy colors rampant. Gastric hunger devouring nourishment needs, akin to slowly creeping vines of anesthetic pitfalls."

Then Stu clarified, "Sour grapes run in your veins."

"I already know I'm my own worst enemy. Can't you tell me something new?"

"You thwart the logarithmic matching-maker malevolently, undermining the dewy drops of dreams, which arrive by every sunrise surprise, only to deadline its demise by your own subterranean sea of fears. Then no dreams can be caught from the fall of stars."

"One more time?" Les asked.

"No matter," the Professor went on. "The question begs to be devalued. Feel the zap. Get charged. Carpe fromaggio. Seize the squeeze!"

All this was not even close to what Les had expected to hear. "But what about the Evolution Accelerator Solution?" he blurted out.

The Professor and Stu looked at each other in silence. Then the Professor reached into his pocket. "Here now, then there, undertake these takers' cupcake coupons." He gave one each to Sir Wintry,

One-Eyed and Les. "Rife with redemption, redeem them as a team or a solo slim jim with Melody at the commensurate cafe fronting outwards."

"You do have an Evolution Accelerator Solution?" Les persisted.

"Oh," the Professor gasped. "My Medley Muffins. I have to back step into their curfew before I burn and banish the allotted lot. That's the oven's truthful, where transformations arise beyond yeasty surmise. Have a musical day!" Then he disappeared through a set of revolving stainless steel doors.

Following the Professor, Stu banged into one of the doors with his power chair. He turned and gave a nervous look, then went through.

"What a total disaster!" Les exclaimed.

"Obviously the Evolution Accelerator Solution is an off-limits topic," Tip Top suggested. "I really thought he would receive you more enthusiastically. I don't know what happened. Sorry to get your hopes up."

"Why did he bother to see me at all if he wasn't going to help me?"

"He did say 'Seize the squeeze,'" suggested Sir Wintry.

"'Ah-ha, ha-ha,'" Les mimicked the Professor. "Big help. This is the last time I put my fate in the hands of a muffin maker. Am I a loser, or what?"

"An aye to that," said One-Eyed teasingly to buoy up Les's spirits. "But we all are, at one time or another."

"Bull's eye," said Tip Top.

"No ice cream without ice," Sir Wintry added.

"No matter," Les mimicked the Professor

again. "I'm a follicle fool in a yo-yo loop. Headline of the day."

"What do you say we all head down to Happy Hour Beach?" One-Eyed asked. "It's that time at the Rebound Bar."

"Happy Hour? I don't believe in it." Les said. "Or happy day, week, month or year. And above all happy life. Bottle that why don't you?"

No one had a response to that.

Then Sir Wintry said, "I'll be glad to drop you off in the limo wherever you like."

"No, you've already done more than enough for me today. Sorry for my outburst. I'm really thankful to all of you. But I prefer to be alone right now."

"Well, let me go ahead and give you my muffin coupon," Sir Wintry said. "I have no need for it."

One-Eyed also gave his coupon to Les. "A drink is what I need for what ails you. Not muffins."

Now Les had three muffin coupons all together. But he didn't feel like going into the cafe to redeem them. That was the farthest thing from his mind. Besides it seemed such a petty gesture on part of the Professor to offer them, especially after the impertinent way he promptly dismissed any talk of the Evolution Accelerator Solution.

Back outside, they said their goodbyes and Les walked alone down the winding road to the sands of Equation Beach.

18   A BLANK SAY

At the beach there were couples, families, and tourists who sat on the sand waiting to watch the sun set over the sea. Les strolled along the water's edge. Soon the darkness would come. He looked up to the east where the sweep of night was already advancing. Of course the Professor was right. Dreams did not fall from the sky. They were not delivered by the stars. No sandman dusted your eyes. Les was the only dreamer in his mind. He was the maker of his own dreams, the maker of his own demise.

So be it. Day by day, sunrise by sunrise, he had journeyed inexorably to this moment of truth. It was time to do away with himself. It was the only proper and fitting tribute to a life lacking a meaningful identity. So the foreboding dark force that he had felt earlier was now revealing its full intent, delivering its final notice. He felt it now, gently like a cloak being draped over him.

One thing he would not do however, was yield to the Blue Sleep. He would not give it the satisfaction. He was going to face his death, yes, but before the Blue Sleep could make its claim upon him. He would stand his ground on that matter. At least in that he could take some small triumphant pride.

Watching the sun slip below the sea's horizon, he felt a certain relief that this would be his last sunset. These would be his last steps on the sands of

Equation Beach. Those would be the last strip of clouds floating violet in the sky that he would see. He felt consoled at the deliberateness with which he took notice of his final observations. No more struggling to fulfill his burdensome longings. He could go in peace.

He walked the rest of the way home, beach after beach, for hours under the moonlight until he came upon the pineapple field that buffered Nameless Beach. He made his way through the plantation and instead of going through the narrow passage that wound its way through the boulders, he climbed up the natural barrier that sheltered his private beach. At the top, he felt a pang of sadness as he took in the overview of his homestead.

But he quickly erased that sentiment and reminded himself that this had been the center of his painful existence. He stoically made his way down, then up to the tree house.

He thought of writing a note. But he realized there was no one to whom he could write. His existence had been a blank, and a blank note was probably the best message he could leave. After all, he had nothing to say.

He thought of putting things in order but things were already in order. He walked through all the levels of the tree house, making a mental note of the details for a final collection of memories to take with him on his final journey.

And then it occurred to him that he had not decided upon the way to end his life, nor the place in which to take his life. It almost made him smile to think he had not thought that through.

Well, considering this was to be his last act as a living being, he might as well choose a dramatic stage. And the most spectacular setting on this part of the island was Melancholy Beach. That was a wild and forbidding place. A perfect place. That's where he would bid farewell to the world.

It would take several hours to get there by foot. He had no time to waste. By leaving at once he would arrive there by sunrise. The end of his life would be an auspicious beginning to the new day.

19 WALLOWING ECSTATIC

Melancholy Beach was a unique site on the island. The county administrators recognized that sometimes, emoticons needed to be alone. They needed a place of solitude, to grieve over some irrevocable loss, or to seek some means to muster the courage to face a doomed outcome, or to find respite from an especially distressing predicament. Thus they designated Melancholy Beach for single-person use only, on a first-come first-serve basis, allowing one-hour maximum usage.

At the trail head that led to the beach, a sign was hung on a wooden post. Prior to embarking down the path, a user was to show the "Occupied" side. Anyone following afterward, was to respect the designation of the sign and refrain from entering. Upon return from the beach, the previous user was to rehang the sign showing the "Vacant" side, to make it available for the next user.

Interestingly enough, as the popularity of the Beach grew, it did not take long for a waiting line of expectant users to form at the signpost. Those awaiting their turn naturally fell into conversations with others in line, as everyone loved to talk about their troubles.

In response to this, the county officials installed benches for those in waiting. To take advantage of this more accommodating setting, people brought their boxed lunches and drinks in ice chests to chat away about their problems while waiting their turn.

The site was also popular with artists, musicians, poets and writers. They found the forsaking landscape of Melancholy Beach inspirational. So the conversations were not necessarily only grievous in nature, but also intensely uplifting, even euphoric.

A young ambitious entrepreneur saw a business opportunity in this phenomenon and received a permit to build The Melancholy Cafe at the signpost location. That way the patrons could lament away, wallowing in their woes, or wax ecstatic about their latest artistic breakthroughs, while sipping on exotic teas and coffees from far away continents, not to mention baked goods from the Professor's Medley Muffin Company. Needless to say, an equally enterprising young woman soon afterward opened The Merrycholy Cafe right next door with similar offerings, including fresh squeezed fruit juices and smoothies.

Thus, ironically enough, it was not uncommon for Melancholy Beach itself to remain vacant and unused for major portions of the day.

When Les arrived at the signpost, it was not yet dawn. The benches were empty. There was no one else about. In the half light of fading night, stars still showed faintly in the sky. Assuming that he was the first person to arrive, he did not bother to look at the signpost to see if it read "Vacant" or "Occupied.'"

He began his walk down the foot path through the dense tropical forest until he came to a small tunnel that bore into the heart of an immense barren stone formation at least ten stories in height. It looked like a massive meteor which had been dropped from the sky at an ancient time. The fierce whistling of the wind nearly sucked him into the tunnel. Feeling his way with his hands upon the narrow walls, he continued until he saw a faint point of light ahead. The ferocity of the wind subsided as the walkway led through a series of ever expanding caves. Soon the sound of waves filled the vast empty spaces.

The path made a sharp turn and suddenly he found himself standing at the center of a magnificent natural band shell facing the violent throes of the chaotic ocean. The half dome filled with the deafening roar of the sea's wild breakers. The waves crashed against an array of jagged rock formations, and the foam shot high into the dawning sky. The turbulent surf surging against the shore sent small rounded stones clattering over one another in metallic chatter.

The beach looked like the wasteland of some apocalyptic geological catastrophe. Les stepped forward to take look at the far edge of the cave to one side. He saw a way for him to climb up to the apex of the cave's overhang which looked to be well over the height of ten stories he had gauged earlier. A jump from that point into the craggy rocks at sea would, without question, promise instant death. Then his body would be washed out to the anonymous waters of the open sea to complete its burial.

The forceful display of the elements in their primeval form gave Les a sense of the astounding power contained in the natural world. And his body, in its deathly state, would become at one with that world. It seemed ironic that in life he only experienced powerlessness and bitterness. Whereas in death, he would become part of the savage grandeur of this awe-inspiring, terrestrial creation.

The sun was now rising, breaking over the distant horizon. It was time to begin his climb.

But before he could take a step, an angry voice from behind shouted, "You're not supposed to be here!"

20 SUNRISE SURPRISE

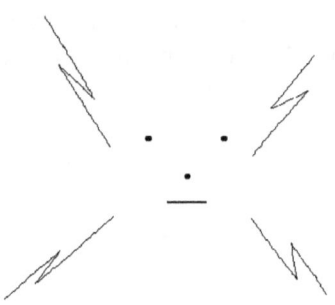

Les turned around and froze on the spot. He felt the charge! In one lightning moment his heart was set aflame. In one world-changing instant, he was utterly, completely, speechlessly smitten. He understood the Professor's prophetic words. The fervent fever. The burning yearning. The converging current. It all made sudden sense. He understood what One-Eyed, Sir Wintry and Tip Top had all been talking about. Before him stood the most ravishing girl he had ever seen, bathed in the glow of the sunrise. Could the Professor have foreseen this surprise?

"Didn't you see the 'Occupied' sign?" she asked, a look of confusion and disappointment on her radiant face.

Despite her expression, the only thing Les

noticed was her beauty, burnished by the first light of day.

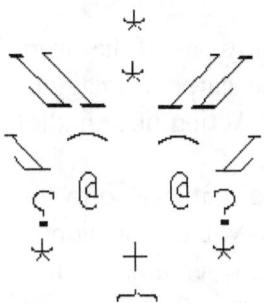

"You're trespassing on my privacy," she said. Les was still too dumbfounded to speak.

"Well?" she asked. "What do you have to say for yourself?"

He could do nothing but absorb her wonder, taking in the vision before him. He noticed she was holding about a dozen white lilies, wrapped in paper imprinted with the words "Equation Beach Florist."

"Are you a deaf-mute?" she asked, her anger softening to self-conscious curiosity.

"Ahhh, er, ahhh. . ." He was too intimidated to form coherent words. She was like some siren from the sea, crushing and fueling his desire at the same time.

"So you can speak?"

"No, I can't." He meant to say that her beauty had rendered him speechless. "I mean, of course, I can, I'm a can."

"You could have fooled me. But this is my designated time here, you know?" Now she talked to him as if he were a child or a demented person. "If you don't follow rules, no one gets alone-time here, and the system falls apart. You understand that, don't you?"

Les nodded foolishly, as if he were in fact demented. This was the carpe fromaggio moment and what was he doing? Acting like an idiot.

"Well?" she asked.

"I'm sorry," Les finally managed to say.

"Fine then. I'll go so you can be alone."

"No!" he wanted to scream. "You can't go. Please don't go." But instead he watched her in silence, as she walked to the water's edge. There she unwrapped the lilies and tossed them into the crashing waves.

Then she came back for a moment. "I trust your day will get better," she said and left.

Les stood still as a stone, watching her disappear. He stared at the face of the half dome cave for a long while, feeling as hollow as the space it shaped. He felt hopeless. Of course that was nothing new. He experienced hopelessness on a daily basis. In fact that was his modus operandi. It was the whole basic premise of his existence.

But no prior hopelessness felt as emptying, as watching this angelic stranger of a girl walk away and disappear from view. He wanted to chase after her. He wanted to beg her to stay. He wanted to know her name, her birthday, where she was born, where she grew up, what was her favorite flavor of ice cream, her favorite song, her favorite. . . flower.

He came out of his shocked revelry and gave chase. He ran as fast as he could shouting "Hello!

Hello!" along the way, his voice echoing back from multiple curved hollows. As he neared the final tunnel, the sudden change from daylight to dimness made him run into its side. He bumped his head and fell down, spraining his ankle. He writhed in pain for a moment. He got up and hopped on one leg, calling out "Hello! Hello!"

By the time he limped down the footpath to the signpost, she was nowhere in sight. The two cafes were still closed. At their front doors stood bundles of newspapers, beverage carts with milk and juices, and stacks of bakery baskets with fresh bread, as well as pastries from The Medley Muffin Company.

Suddenly he remembered the wrapping paper with the imprint "Equation Beach Florist." He had a lead. He could go there. They might know her. Maybe she was a regular customer. He would wait for her there, every day if need be, until she appeared. He had to find her again.

"Wait a minute, you follicle fool!" his mind's self-talk interjected. "You lopsided anomaly, you nebula of navel lint. What exactly are you going to do if you do find her? She was right here, right in front of you, and what did you do? Nothing. And you know what you're going to do if you do find her at the flower shop? Again nothing. Absolutely nothing. Because you're only a fractured fraction, just like the Professor said. You haven't even got a braille backhand. So what's the point? You're the same old you, acting like the same old you, getting nowhere like the same old you. So remember why you came here in the first place. Finish the deed. Go back to the beach, climb up the side of the cave, get to the top and throw yourself over."

"No," Les objected against his own mind. "I'm not listening to you. I have to see her again. I'm going to see her again. And when I do see her, it won't be as the old me. I'm going back to the Professor to get that Evolution Accelerator Solution. Even if I have to beg, borrow or steal. I'm going to fight for it. I didn't fight for it before because I wasn't worth fighting for. But this girl is worth fighting for. And I'll win her over. Not as me. But as a new me. I will become somebody she can't refuse. Today the old Les dies. Tomorrow I will be the new Super-Les!"

21 CONFUSING HAPPINESS

By the time Les arrived at the bakery-laboratory, it was late morning. He went to the back and rang the service bell button. Tip Top raised the roll-up door to greet him. "You're back," he said.

"I felt the zap," Les declared, all smiles.

"What?"

"I felt the charge."

"What charge?"

"Angela, Blossom, Serena."

"Oh, that charge," Tip Top returned the smile. "What a surprise. Who's the lucky girl?"

"I don't know."

"You don't know?"

"No."

"I'm confused."

"No matter. I'm here to see the Professor."

"Wait, if it's about the Evolution Accelerator Solution, that's a no-go. Remember how it went yesterday?"

"Today is a brand new day. I met the girl of my dreams. But I can't approach her as me you see? She hates me."

"Already? You work fast. What did you do to her?"

"Nothing."

"And that's why she hates you?"

"I don't have time to explain. It's very confusing happiness. I just need to see the Professor."

"I'm already in hot water with him for telling you about the Solution. I only did it because you fit the profile for the candidate's list."

"What candidate's list?"

"Well, actually there is no list."

"You just said there was."

"There is, but there's no one on the list yet."

"But you thought I could make the list?"

"Yes, well, I was afraid if I told you why, you might get upset. I didn't want to embarrass you, or hurt your feelings."

"How?"

"Okay, fine. Just don't tell me I don't care about your feelings. The Evolution Accelerator Solution works best on a person with no personality, no strength of character, no significant talents, no superior skill sets, no individually distinguishing features. Those characteristics would naturally resist the effects of the formula. In short, it needs a plain and simple nobody."

"That's great news! So I'm good for something. I'm a perfect match!"

"Bull's eye! That's why I brought you here. I thought the Professor would be thrilled with me. But as you saw, he wasn't overjoyed at all. And I don't know why."

"So?"

"So I can't let you see him. I can't take a chance on upsetting him again."

"But if I'm the best candidate?"

"Sorry, Les. I can't forsake my standing with the Professor. Here," and Tip Top handed Les another coupon.

"I already have three of these at home," Les said.

"One more won't hurt. Get yourself a doughnut or a muffin, some cupcakes. You look starved. Just go around the building to the cafe in the front. Melody will take care of you. Now I've got to make an urgent delivery for an order that just came in. And good luck with that girl you don't know. Hope you find her soon."

Tip Top went out, got into a van and drove off.

Les decided this was his chance. He would search the premises, upstairs, downstairs, in the cellar, the attic, until he found Professor Sequel. As he started to go through a set of double doors, he was startled by a power chair that nearly rammed him. It was Stu Harking, blocking his way.

"Where do you think you're going?" Stu asked. "This area is for authorized personnel only."

"I know and I'm sorry, but I have to see the Professor. It's very urgent. My life depends on it."

"Are you dying?"

"I may as well die if I don't get help."

"Are you ill?"

"No, I'm fine. Look, it's complicated. And the Professor is the only one who can help me."

"I must have a sampling of your blood."

"What?"

"The Professor suffers from a unique malady. Too complicated for you to understand. He is susceptible to certain infections. I have to examine your blood to make sure you're not carrying anything that might have infected him in anyway during your last visit."

"What about One-Eyed and Sir Wintry? Have you taken their blood?"

"They will be contacted at the appropriate time."

"And I need to contact the Professor, now."

"I know why you're here. You want the Evolution Accelerator Solution. Unfortunately, the Professor destroyed it long ago."

"What? But Tip Top just told me I was the best candidate for it."

"Tip Top's behind the times. The Professor's been on a different research path for a while now. So you see, it's quite pointless for you to seek audience with him."

Les was dumbfounded. He had pinned his hopes on the EAS and now it didn't even exist. How was he going to win the girl of his dreams now?

"This way," Stu directed.

Les was so crestfallen from the shocking news, that he offered no resistance.

He followed Stu into a room that looked like a combination medical clinic and science laboratory. Stu quickly and efficiently drew a test tube full of blood from Les. Then Stu gave Les a card with his phone number on it and said, "Call me in a few days." Then Stu escorted Les out the back entrance.

Les felt lost. He had to take a moment to get his bearings. Without the Evolution Accelerator Solution he had no hope. He was back down in the depths of despair.

But wait, he could still go down to the flower shop at least and make an inquiry. Then what? Even if he found out her whereabouts, he didn't have the confidence to approach her as himself.

One step at a time, he told himself. First grab some muffins with the coupon, then maybe by the time he got to the flower shop some strategy would pop into his head. He couldn't give up so easily on a girl like that. He would never find anyone like her again.

22   COUPON ENCOUNTER

Les went around the building to the front. He saw a fold-out sign with the name "Medley Brunch Cafe" printed on it. The opening hours were also posted. The sign was set on the marble floor of the spacious patio brightly lit by the sun. Tall antebellum columns cast shadows across the tables--each decorated with a vase of lilies. Four sets of double doors were drawn wide open, giving the interior an airy feeling. A few tables were already occupied by customers.

A waitress carrying a tray of items passed by him. "Hallo, my name Yolanda. I come back, help you in one moment."

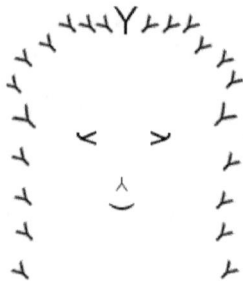

Before Les could utter a reply, she hurried away to serve her customers. Then in the next moment another waitress approached Les from behind. "Good day. I am Esmeralda. You want table or takeaway?"

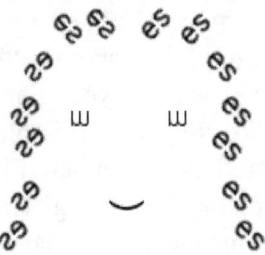

"I was told by Tip Top that a Melody would take care of me."

"Yes, she over there," Esmeralda said, pointing to a girl at the counter with her back to them.

Les thanked Esmeralda and approached the girl who was polishing the cappuccino-espresso machine with a hand cloth.. "Excuse me," Les said. "I have a coupon."

When the girl turned around, Les felt thunderstruck. It was the girl from Melancholy Beach! She was right here. The search was over. He didn't need to go to the flower shop.

"It's you again," she said, looking defensive with her elbows out and fists clenched at her hips. "What are you, some kind of a stalker? This can't be a coincidence."

Les was speechless. He held the coupon out to her.

She took it from him begrudgingly and said, "Fine. So, you have several choices. Any two items from the shelves here on the left, or three items from the shelves on the right. Or, if you want the jackpot, any five items from that big basket there at the end of the counter. They're from yesterday but still moist and full of flavor. For here or to go?"

"For here," he wanted to shout. "And I'm staying forever. I'm never leaving you. For the rest of my life I'll be here. I will die in this place, this very spot." But of course Les remembered he was a nobody, who had no chance with a girl like her, until he changed into someone else, so he said, "To go."

And he was immediately disappointed with himself. Why did he always do the opposite of what he really wanted to do? He had an important message for her. He wanted to tell her that she had saved his life, that she had kept him from throwing himself off the cave-top cliff. If it weren't for her, his body would be at the bottom of the ocean in rock-ripped pieces. She had interrupted his death and his soul was full of infinite gratitude. But he was unable to tell her any of these things. Instead he kept it all inside him, intimidated by her hostility. He had to wait for a better time.

She handed him a take-out bag and asked, "Anything to drink?"

"Is that included?"

"Only if you never come back again."

Ouch! That really hurt. Les felt like he was being stabbed in the heart by one of Tip Top's arrows. He felt like a stunt kite shot to the ground. Didn't the Better Business Bureau have policies against service personnel talking to a customer like this?

"I'll have a bottle of sparkling water," Les said.

"Coming right up," she said, turning to the glass-door refrigerator behind her.

Les used the self-service tongs to place a strawberry muffin, a cinnamon roll and a chocolate croissant into the take-out bag.

"Here you are," she said, handing him the bottle.

"Thanks," Les said. And then there was nothing else to do. He was facing a vacant moment. And he had no idea how to fill it. If only he had said he wanted a table. Then he could have sat for hours, watching her work. He would have been in heaven. But it was too late now. She had told him to leave and never come back.

"Thanks again," Les said. "I'll go now."

"Best move you can make," she said.

As he turned and left, he felt as if the fire in her eyes were boring a burning hole through his back.

23   SEEING EYE CAT

Les certainly did not want to leave but he had already committed himself to leaving. And now his legs were carrying him away despite his heart's desire to remain. This was exactly the kind of thing that upset him about himself. He always managed to do the converse of his true intentions. What a show of incompetence.

Not only that, he had found his dream girl and been totally rejected by her. Actually, she was not his dream girl because he had not dared to dream about a girl as stunning and ravishing as Melody. But strangely enough, the moment he saw her, it felt as if had indeed dreamed about her. He felt as if he recognized her, even though he had never seen her before. It was as if the heart knew who she was to him before he knew it himself.

However, obviously his heart was mistaken because she had not wanted anything to do with him. If she were truly his dream girl, wouldn't she also have recognized that he was her dream man? But that sounded ridiculous. How could he be a dream man to any girl? So he was right back where he started. A nobody going nowhere, doing nothing for himself and regretting it.

What a roller coaster ride of events. One minute he was flying high on his dream of becoming the world's first Super-Emoticon, to win over the great love of his life. The next minute, he was falling to the depressing depths of being a nobody again, with no chance to claim the girl who stole his heart. He felt exhausted and emotionally drained.

Now he wished he hadn't met her at all. Seeing her had filled him with false hope. In fact, he was feeling somewhat upset with her for interrupting his plan to end his life. If it hadn't been for her, he'd be dead. Happily dead. Peacefully dead. And he wouldn't have to deal with the current state of events. The super-emoticon dream was dead. The winning-the-girl plan was dead. There was only one thing left to do.

Les took the bus back to Melancholy Beach to fulfill his original plan. Unfortunately the sign at the trail head indicated "Occupied." He took a seat on one of the waiting benches. The two cafes across the way were already full. As he finished off his bottle of water, he had a sneaky suspicion that those people sipping their cappuccinos and smoothies were not really melancholy. They were pretenders to melancholy. He was the only true melancholy.

Little did they know that he was about to take his life again. None of them were surely going to take their lives within the hour. They were enjoying their drinks and conversations too much to be intending death.

Les took out his chocolate croissant from his bag and told himself this was going to be the very last chocolate croissant he was ever going to eat. It would be one of his last conscious acts. So he wanted to pay close attention to every bite.

Suddenly a weary looking old man sat down next to Les and said, "Full house."   He was referring to the two cafes.

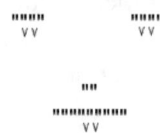

Les merely nodded, since his mouth was full of pastry.

"What ails ya?" the old man asked.

Les was annoyed. He wanted his full attention on the chocolate croissant. But that was the problem with going out in public. There was always a chance some stranger was going to come up to you out of nowhere and start a conversation.

What a nightmare. He was in no mood for a conversation. He was on a mission to kill himself and he wanted to go about it in the proper way. There were certain protocols to follow. And this stranger was ruining everything.

"You got troubles?" the old man asked, leaning so close to Les's face that their noses were almost touching.

"Here," Les said, opening up his bag. "Have a cinnamon roll." The ruse to create some facial separation from the old man worked.

"Much obliged," the old man smiled. He began chewing on the pastry with his mouth open. Crumbs fell onto his chest.

Les felt as if he had somehow betrayed Melody. These pastries were from the cafe where she worked. As such, they had an aura of beatific reverence. They were, after all, offered to him by his dream girl, or more truthfully, his ex-dream girl. They were blessed with her exquisiteness. And here he was sharing them with an old man who ate like an insect.

"So what ails ya?" the old man asked again with food particles showing between his teeth.

Les did not want to open up his heart to a stranger. He did not want to tell him how he had been utterly rejected by Melody. He did not want to tell him he was performing the last rites of a private ritual suicide. Luckily for Les, the old man did not wait to get a reply.

"Too choked up about it, are ya?" the old man guessed, misinterpreting Les's silence. Then he burped loudly and said, "Let me tell ya 'bout my troubles." He reached into Les's bag and asked, "Mind if I have the muffin too?"

"Be my guest," Les said reluctantly, as if he were giving up a precious jewel to a thief.

The old man talked and chewed at the same time. "I'm goin' blind." Then he paused, waiting for a consoling word from Les.

When Les realized this after a prolonged silence, he said, "Oh, I'm sorry."

"Yeah," the old man sighed. "Gonna have to get myself a seeing-eye dog. But the kicker of it is, I hate dogs. Can't stand 'em. Never had one. Never wanted one. Don't feel like gettin' one. But I gotta. Can ya' imagine that? I'm a cat person. Got a whole slew of cats. But they don't make seein' eye cats. And my cats are gonna raise hell when I bring a dog home. See my predicamen'?"

"Yes, I do."

"I got troubles."

"Yes, you do."

"Nobody else got my predicamen'."

"No, you're right."

"Know anybody with my predicamen'?"

"No, I'm afraid I don't. Although, I do have a friend who only has one good eye. He wears a patch over the other. "

"Aint' the same predicamen'."

"No, it's not . . ." And suddenly Les had a eureka moment. The image of One-Eyed Lax and his eye-patch gave him an idea. All was not lost with his dream-girl Melody after all. His suicide would have to wait one more day. He had a plan that did not require any kind of super potion.

"Hey, fella," the old man nudged Les with his elbow. "A table jus' opened up. We can have a sit, you and me."

Les got up and shook the old man's hand vigorously with a smile. He no longer looked like an insect. He looked like a wise old Buddha who had helped Les arrive at an enlightened moment. "Thanks," Les said. "But I just remembered some errands I have to run. And I enjoyed our chat. Good bye."

And just like that, all was right with the world again.

24   A SLEEPING COINCIDENCE

By the time Les finished shopping for an eye-patch, it was late afternoon. He knew the Medley Cafe was closed by now. He would have to wait until morning to see Melody. That was fine by him for he was truly exhausted and needed a good night's rest.

Back at home, Nameless Beach suddenly looked like paradise. It was Melody's doing. Even though she wasn't here in person, her presence in the world gave his domain a remarkable luster.

He ate a hearty meal and slept in the hammock under the moon and the stars. He couldn't be bothered to give a single thought about the Blue Sleep. He felt on the verge of a triumph.

In the morning, he arose to the rising sun, took a swim in the sea, had a grand breakfast, showered and got dressed. He knew he could not face Melody as himself. But he could go incognito. He could go in disguise. He would go as "One-Eyed Les."

He looked at himself in the mirror and smiled. The eye-patch instantly gave him a wickedly different feeling. He felt a sudden rush of freedom. He felt he could do things that the real Les Dan Nil could never do. It emboldened him.

He was a man in love and everything seemed possible, especially now as an imposter. Pretending to be somebody else gave him a sense of power he had not known before. It was going to be an unforgettable, brave new day.

When he arrived at Medley Cafe, Melody was wiping down the counter. She looked different, but it was unmistakably her.

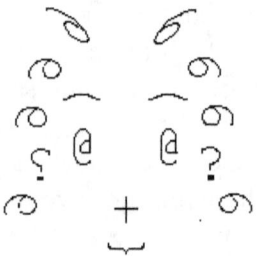

Just to confirm his certainty, he asked, "It is you, isn't it?"

"Who else would I be?"

"No one."

"Nice to know."

Les winced. Why couldn't his words ever match his thoughts whenever he was around her?

"No. I mean, no one could be you."

"Thank the stars for that. The world doesn't need another me. But you. Is there another you?"

"I'm sorry?"

"Usually, the way the world works, there's only one version of everybody. But you look familiar."

Les began to panic. Did she already see through his disguise? "Ah, er, I'm the only one of me I know. But probably, maybe, most likely, you've seen me at Happy Hour Beach."

"Never go there. I love the Wonder Mile Walkway though. Are you a regular at the Double H?"

"No, been there only once."

"That would have to be a big coincidence."

"What?"

"For me to have seen you there if you've been there only once."

"Yes. You're right. One chance in once."

"Your voice sounds familiar too."

Les flinched. He could not think fast enough for her. He had not properly prepared himself for this kind of dialogue. Why did his simple idea turn out to be so difficult to carry out? He began to perspire. "You must be thinking of someone else."

"It wouldn't be the first time. What happened to your eye, if I'm not being too personal?"

"Ah, I don't seem to recollect."

"You don't remember how you hurt your eye?"

Now Les was in big trouble. He didn't realize he would have to have a cover story. He didn't know she was going to give him the third degree. He thought of telling her One-Eyed Lax's story. But he didn't want to dishonor Serena's memory. Besides, having never had a girlfriend, he didn't think his acting abilities were good enough to achieve the required emotional truth of a tragic loss of love.

Furthermore, he wasn't impersonating One-Eyed Lax. He was impersonating "One-Eyed Les," which meant he would have to have a completely different history from One-Eyed Lax. Unable to come up with anything plausible on such short notice, he blurted out, "It was a coincidence."

"Of injury?"

"Yes, it happened in my sleep."

"How awful."

"Yes, and I passed out."

"In your asleep?" She was now talking to him like a child, as if she saw through his ruse and was playing along for her amusement.

"Yes. Immediately. Before I knew it." In a state of nervousness, he began to blink furiously, looking in all directions, unable to look at her directly.

"Don't you remember anything else?" She gave him a sly look.

His mind totally blocked, he heard himself say, "I have a coupon."

She took it from him and slapped it on top of the counter. "I knew it was you," she said with a stern look. "And take off that ridiculous eye patch."

Les hesitated. He wanted to run away. He couldn't face her as his usual self. That would be too painful, too embarrassing. He needed the eye-patch to hide his real self.

"Take it off." Her voice was so assertive, so

commanding, he had to obey. He removed it and placed it on the counter.

She promptly threw it in the trash. "I'm obligated to honor your coupon, so here's your bag. Take whatever you want from any shelf you want, as much as you want. But if you come back here again I will call the police."

Completely devastated, ashamed and humiliated, Les started filling his bag mindlessly. Fortunately another customer came up to the counter requiring Melody's attention. So Les was able to slip out of the Cafe like a silent, cowardly thief.

Now he was right back where he started again. This new day which had begun so auspiciously, suddenly seemed too much like the day before. Why continue to punish himself with these rejections? It was clear she was not attracted to him. She did not care about him. She had no civil feelings for him. Even as her customer, he was persona non grata.

The only option was to go back to his original plan. But this time he would do it at home. He didn't want to take a chance on some Buddha-like stranger changing his mind for him again. No, this time, he would go quietly to his death in the solitary tranquility of his Nameless Beach.

25   WADDLING BUDDHA

On the way home, Les was so absorbed in his depressing thoughts that he missed his bus stop. In fact he had ridden all the way to the Melancholy Beach stop before he realized where he was. He got off just in time. Now there was a half hour wait for the return bus.

Les decided to take his bag of pastries to the Melancholy Waiting Benches. Although the various rolls, muffins and cupcakes were anointed with Melody's aura, that beatific quality no longer felt personal. Let someone else enjoy the magic of her emanation, he thought.

It was clear she could never develop any feelings for him. He was just another customer. No, not even that. A customer she would want to see again. She certainly did not want his return. So he was held in a lower regard than a customer. Another confirmation of his general lowly status.

Both Melancholy and Merrycholy cafes were full. And already some people were sitting on the Waiting Benches. But one was vacant. However before Les reached it, an enormous woman waddling like a duck grabbed him by the arm. She was breathing heavily and perspiring profusely. Even her palms were wet.

"Oh, Lordy," she said, leaning heavily upon Les. "Be a jennelman. I gotta set myself down 'fore I fall and die. I be so tired."

Les struggled with his balance as he guided her

to the empty bench. Her perspiration transferred onto his shirt and arms. Les was not pleased. This was exactly why he shied away from going out in public. All kinds of negative pleasantries could befall him. How he wished he were home now.

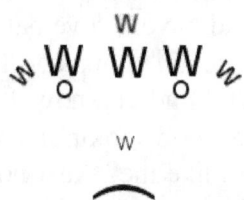

The woman sat down, then took out a big handkerchief and wiped her under arms. "I'm in a stinkin' mess," she said. "Oh, lordy, a big ol' mess o' my own makin'. Wat I gonna do? I'm askin' ya', wat I gonna do?"

Les wanted to run. However, considering the crowd at both cafes and the other benches, he felt it would be unseemly for him to leave this woman stranded. So in his most polite voice he asked, "What seems to be the trouble?"

"I gotta man comin' to see me. He comin' on a airoplane tomorrow! But I cain't see him. No, suh. No way, no how. I'd ratha die den him see me like dis."

"Why? Who is he?"

"He the love o' my life. He my dream man. Oh lordy lordy, he such a good lookin' man. I got his picture. He sent it first thing. Mighty fine picture.

Just makes me wanna lick his eyes they so beautiful, you know what I mean? When you look into a man's eyes you see sumpin. He's my man, I know it. But I caint see him no way. Uh, uh. When he see my big ass butt, he gonna run. He never gonna come back. He gonna stop writin'. And I gonna lose him for shure. Then what I gonna do? He the best pen pal I ever did have. I love dat man. But he aint gonna love me. He ain't gonna go for no fat ellyfant like me. I ain't blind. I know I be a whale. How in the world a good lookin' man like him go for a hippomamasass like me? Ain't no way dat gonna happen. No suh."

"You mean he doesn't know what you look like?"

"O, dat my mistake. He kept askin' an' askin' for a picture. I hold him off as long as I could. But finally, an' everybody told me don' do no such ting. Don' be lyin', girl. But I sent him picture o' my sister. She so beautiful nobody can believe we's sisters. Nobody in our fam'ly or even our relations-- everybody wondrin' where she come from? How God put an angel like her in our fam'ly? She the sweetest ting. I love her to death. She so good, dat girl. She ain't no lyin' cheat like me, foolin' a pen pal dream man. Oh, he gonna kill me when he come tomorrow. Spendin' all dat money on a airoplane. He gonna be cussin' up and down all o' Emoticonda, he is. Oh, he gonna kill me."

"If he's as good a man as you say he is . . . "

"O, he a very good man. He make me so hot and bothered in his letters you know. He get me so excited. He get me goin' so helpless I jus' have to run to the kitchin' an' have myself a piece o' chocolate pecan pie. And I make the best chocolate pecan pie in da ailand. Dat the truth. Take me three or four pieces to cool down from his letters. O, dat man. He be my man fo' sho'. But he ain't gonna love me when he see me. No, he ain't. You see why I cryin'? I been cryin' all night."

Les wished he could help the woman. He wished he could comfort her somehow. But her problem was so alien to his own that he could think of nothing appropriate. And he felt secretly guilty for the thought that had occurred to him while he was listening to her story. Something clicked in his mind when she mentioned the word "pen pal." It was another eureka moment.

He knew right away what he had to do. He would write Melody a letter. Then he could finally express his gratitude to her for saving his life that day at Melancholy Beach. With that accomplished, he could go ahead and die. But of course he could not deliver the letter himself. He would have to use another disguise. And he did have two more coupons.

Les looked at the woman again, feeling ashamed for having personally benefited with another light-bulb moment from her sad tale. Nevertheless he was filled with benevolence and gratitude for the inadvertent moment of enlightenment. So this time, Buddha came not in the form of an insect, but a waddling 'ellyfant.' Les was impressed with Buddha's repertoire of identities.

"I have some muffins," he said, offering her the bag of pastries. "Take the whole thing."

"O, lordy. Ain't you kind. Dis be like my birthday. I jus' might have myself a party now. Which one your favorite?"

"Oh, no, none for me. I've had enough. Besides I have to run. But you know, your pen pal, he'd be crazy not to marry you. I mean he's in love with the you that wrote those letters, right? You put your heart and soul into your words. But if he's only interested in some picture, he's not worth it."

"Ain't you a darlin'. But who knows? Maybe you see me killed dead here tomorrow by my dream man. Maybe you read about it in the papers. Lordy, I don' know what I gonna do. But these mighty fine muffins. Almost good as my chocolate pecan pie."

26 MUFFIN BLINDNESS

The next day, Les waited until the afternoon to go to the Medley Cafe. For one thing he had to work out an extensive cover story for his new persona in disguise. For another, he wanted to be at the Cafe when there were plenty of customers. Then perhaps Melody would be more civil to him. Thus Les put on Sir Wintry's sunglasses and named himself, Sir Lesheart.

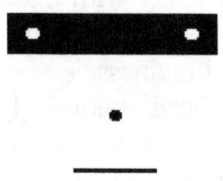

Once again, he enjoyed looking at himself with another identity. It was easier to deal with the world as someone else other than himself. Unfortunately, it was only a temporary identity, and the benefits were also only temporary. If only he could have found a way to make a permanent identity change.

When he arrived at the Cafe, Melody once again looked curiously different. But he knew it was her.

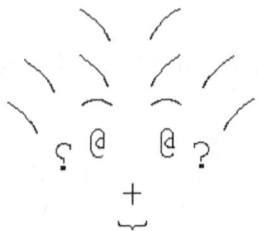

He greeted her with a smile. "Good afternoon, Miss."

"You look familiar."

This time Les was ready with his cover story. "These glasses perhaps. I suffer from a rare and advanced form of snow blindness."

She nodded her head knowingly. "Funny, there's a Sir Wintry who has the same condition. One of our best customers. Do you happen to know him?"

"Indeed. He is a distant relation."

"You don't say?"

"I'm a long lost step brother to his adopted second cousin on his foster grandmother's side by an annulled third marriage. Sir Cubeheart himself of course has no awareness of our common ancestry. And in respect to his fame and fortune, I prefer not to flaunt our rare and special shared lineage publicly." Les impressed himself with such a quick response. He did his homework. He had an airtight cover story.

"That explains the resemblance."

"Quite. I have been entrusted to act as an envoy for a personal acquaintance. I humbly submit this billet-doux." He handed her the envelope.

"Who is this from?"

"Les Dan Nil. A charming man. Quite simpatico."

"I'm afraid I don't know anyone by that name. Are you sure I'm the right person?"

"Indeed. Make no mistake about it. You are so perfect, I mean, the right so person, er so right person."

"Strange . . . And what is your name?"

"Sir Lesheart."

"So you're a knight as well?"

"It would be an honor to regale you with the tale of how I came to acquire that title."

"Haven't the time. But tell me more about this friend of yours. Why couldn't he come here himself?"

Oh, oh. Les was beginning to have a panic attack. He had worked on a cover story for the Sir Lesheart identity, but he had not worked out a cover story for himself as himself.

"Ah, hem. Yes. He was temporarily indisposed."

"Because of?"

Les had not counted on her asking about the real Les at all. He was in a spot now. He had no time to fabricate a fictitious past for himself. Think! The clock is ticking. The silence is growing. Say something. Anything. Just break the silence. Darn. If only she would ask him more questions about Sir

Lesheart.

"Wouldn't you prefer to inquire about my past?" Les implored. "I have led such a colorful life."

"No, thanks. You're just the messenger."

"Ah, yes. In addition to my duty as envoy, I am to collect a sampling of your delicious offerings. I have a coupon."

"I knew it." She slapped the coupon on the counter. "That's the giveaway. Three strikes now and you're out."

Then she ripped the envelope and the coupon and threw both in the trash.

Les was crushed. He had opened up his wounded heart in writing the letter, confessing his unbounded gratitude for her immaculate presence at Melancholy Beach which had saved his life. And now that precious letter was in the waste basket. It felt as if his heart also lay there, torn and disposed by the girl he loved.

"I cannot believe you came back again!" she said angrily. "And take those silly glasses off or I will personally give you muffin blindness."

Les did so, feeling defeated once again.

She promptly dropped them in the waste basket. Then she took the largest jumbo sized bag and filled it with all manner of fresh pastries—rolls, buns, muffins, tarts, kringles, bear claws, plain croissants, chocolate croissants, jelly rolls, palmiers, pain au raisins and so on. There was enough pastry to feed two cafes full of people. "Is Les Dan Nil your real name?" she demanded.

"Yes."

"I'm going to give that name to the police if you show your face here again, disguised or undisguised. Do you understand?"

"Yes, but if you'll let me explain . . ."

"I've heard enough from you. I know you're a liar and an imposter." She handed him the giant bag of pastries. "Now go away and never come back. That's your final warning!"

27 BROTHER IN HARM

Depressed and despondent Les boarded the bus at the Equation Beach bus stop. He was somewhat taken aback when the bus driver smiled and said, "I can't believe it. You get a free ride today."

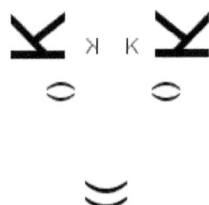

Les looked behind him to see if the bus driver was talking to someone else. But there was no one.

"Where are you going with all those pastries?" the bus driver asked.

"Home."

"They all for yourself?"

"Well . . . "

"I'll buy them from you, right here. Right now."

"I don't understand."

"Sit down."

Les took the front seat.

"Thank God you showed up. Listen. My brother works as a waiter at the Merrycholy Cafe and they ran out of these goodies. The Medley

Muffin Company doesn't make deliveries in the afternoons. Only mornings. So the manager of the cafe sent my brother to make a run to the bakery and surprise, surprise, I almost ran him over on his scooter just a while ago. I didn't expect to see him out on the road because he's supposed to be working. So I honked to make sure it was him and he panicked and fell over, sprained his wrist, banged up his elbow, got a couple of scratches and bruises. Nothing serious, but he's done for the day. Maybe couple of days."

"Sorry to hear that."

"Don't be sorry. You're the answer to my prayers."

"I am?"

"Listen, I gotta make it up to my brother. Let me buy everything in the bag. Cash. And I'll even pay you to make a quick run to the Cafe when I make my stop at Melancholy Beach. I'll hold the bus till you come back. Take you where you wanna go after that."

Not again. That's what happens when you go out in the world. You get caught up in some stranger's tall tale and you're stuck like a moth in a spider's web. That's why he liked staying home. Nothing unforeseen happens when you're home. You know exactly what's coming. No surprises. The day goes nice and smooth without any intrusive demands made by strangers.

Les sighed and said, "You don't have to pay me." And then he lied, "I was going there anyway."

"You sure? I got money."

"No. It's all right. I don't need money."

"Everybody needs money. Makes the world go round."

"Well, I'm not going around the world anytime soon."

"You're definitely doing your good deed for the day. And it's a whopper. Thanks a million!"

When Les was dropped off, he told the driver not to wait. Then he made his delivery to the Merrycholy Cafe where the manager first expressed dismay at the news of her waiter, then gratitude to Les for the baked goods. In fact, the manager offered him a cafe coupon but Les declined.

He decided he might as well stay and take his life here and now instead of going home. There was no reason to go back to Nameless Beach. He looked at the signpost at the head of the footpath and it showed "Occupied." There were seats available at both cafes but he took a seat on an empty bench closest to the sign.

As he waited for his appointment with death, he looked at the distant scenery, avoiding eye contact with the cafe customers. When he did inadvertently look their way, he noticed one lady with bushy blonde eyebrows staring at him. Her eyes had a special permanent sparkle. He quickly looked away, pretending he didn't notice. But when he looked back, she smiled at him.

For a moment he thought she was smiling at someone else, but there was no one beside him. That unnerved him to no end. For the rest of his waiting period he sat tensely looking in all directions at unfocused distances.

Finally, he let out a sigh of relief when the prior

occupant of the beach appeared out of the trail and turned the sign around to the "Vacant" side. However, as soon as Les got up to reach for the sign, the staring woman came up and snatched it out of his hand. That's when he noticed her unmistakable blonde mustache.

28   NAKED AT THE EDGE

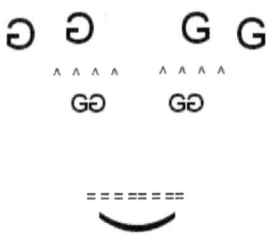

"Oh, I'm sorry, honey," the woman said. "But I'm next. I was waiting at the cafe, you see." In the other hand she was carrying a large portfolio case.

Les was so flabbergasted he could only stand there speechless.

She was a middle-aged woman in a tank top and a pair of shorts, who reeked of tobacco. She looked somewhat androgynous. Being blonde, her mustache did not show from a distance, but face to face, Les could not miss it. He wondered why she didn't shave it off. But then again, her underarms were also unshaven, as well as her legs.

"I thought the official waiting was done on the benches," Les protested.

"A silly little rule, don't you think?"

"Well, I suppose I can wait a little longer."

"Thanks, honey. I knew you'd be nice. Actually, if you'd like, we can go together."

"The rule is one person at a time."

"I hate rules like that, don't you?"

"Well, I don't feel comfortable . . ."

"You'd be doing me a big favor."

"I'm sorry?"

"I've been watching you. And I was suddenly struck by an inspirational thought. I think you're just what I need."

"I don't understand."

"I'm an artist. Working with pastels today. This beach is like my white whale. I've tried and tried to get it right, to do justice to it, to capture all that wild unbridled force of nature on such stunning display, only to fail every single time. But when I saw you on the bench looking so plain and simple, I realized you'd be perfect to put in my drawing. I need a subject as a contrast to all that elemental power of the wailing sea, the tortured formations of the caves, and the suffering desolate stones. You wouldn't have to do anything special. I just need a nondescript anonymous figure. And you're definitely that."

Thanks a lot, Les thought. Now he regretted not going home. Once again he was ensnared into participating in the life of a stranger. And he could not think of any appropriate reasons to back out. He disliked himself for not having the power to say 'no.'

"But what about the people at the cafe?" Les inquired. " They'll see us go in together."

"Let them think the worst. What do you care?"

That was true. It occurred to Les that he was going to die in a matter of hours. It was time to adopt a devil may care attitude. He was leaving this world. He would never see these people again. He didn't care what they thought. Besides, after she finished her drawing, she would be on her way. Then he could simply stay at the beach and take his life.

"You're right," he said. "I don't care. I don't care about anything."

"Oooh, you're such a rebel. You're giving me goose bumps now. Let's go."

Once at the beach, facing the sea, their voices nearly drowning in the roar of the waves, she opened up her case full of pastels, drawing paper and drawing board. .

"Where do I stand?" Les asked.

"I'm not sure yet. But I have to ask you one thing. I need you to take your clothes off."

"What?"

"Don't worry. I'm not going to attack you. I'm old enough to be your mother. It would make a more powerful statement if you were nude against the elements, you know?"

"I've never . . . "

"There's nobody here. Just you and me. What do you care?"

Once again, she was right. He didn't care. That was the one big advantage of knowing you were going to die in a matter of hours. It made you carefree. It made you brave. It made you feel ferocious and invincible. How paradoxical was that?

He did as she asked. And as she went back to her spot to draw, Les stood naked at the edge of the formidable sea, on a roughly hewn rock just inches away from the onslaught of the waves. He braced himself against the fury of the wind that threatened to cast him into the deadly waters.

Time flew in a timeless manner as Les lost himself, calm and centered amidst the savage terrestrial rage running rampant all around him. He felt infused by the power of the cosmic forces. He felt fearless. And he realized, in a wave crashing moment that he could take this fearlessness to confront Melody once more

Yes, he would postpone his death for one more day, again. He was seized by the moment. In turn, he would seize the day. He had something to say to Melody. And he would have his say no matter what. Let her call the police. What could they do to him? He was already a dead man. And what could Melody do? The barbs and darts of her rejection could not hurt him any longer. The dead could not die twice.

At sunset, the mustached lady told him she was done. "Thank you so much. I finally got what I wanted."

"It was nothing," Les said.

"You don't know how frustrated I've been with this place. At one point I was so tormented by my failures that I came here with bottles and bottles of pre-mixed water colors and splashed them against the rocks, the waves, the sand and stones. I wanted to prove that I could paint this place. Too bad it wasn't on canvas. So it was a Pyrrhic victory. It sent me into a deep depression. But eventually I got past that and today I came back. I'm so glad you were here. You turned out to be the missing element. I'm very happy with what I accomplished today. In fact, when I get home, I'm calling some friends over and celebrate with champagne and cigars!"

So Buddhas not only come with mustaches and thick tufts of underarm hair, Les thought. They also drink champagne and smoke cigars. Les was once again grateful for Buddha's infinite incarnations. He shook her hand warmly and left.

29 SUNRISE REPRISE

Les spent the next three days preparing for his final visit to see Melody. On the fourth day he arrived at Equation Beach in a hot air balloon. He had fashioned himself after Tip Top Burrows. In addition, he wore a medieval archer's costume, complete with a quiver of arrows across his back and a bow over one shoulder.

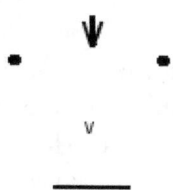

Sunbathing tourists on the beach scrambled away to make space for the balloon's landing. As it descended to the sands, Les unrolled a banner with the following lines:

Though lilies were banished to the sea
you came to rescue me--
I'm that grateful stranger at the shore
who lived to feast on muffins once more!

Naturally the spectacle drew the interest of the customers at the Medley Cafe higher up the bluff. As he expected, Melody was also taking a look. Her dismayed frown did not deter Les from continuing.

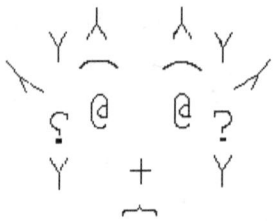

When it was clear that Melody had read the banner message, Les dropped it on the beach just before the balloon touched ground. He picked up a kite, put it under his arm and waved boldly to Melody.

She merely placed her fists on her hips, a gesture he had seen from her far too often.

Undaunted by her hostile response, he ran down the beach to set the kite flying into the air. It had a long wide tail with a printed message:

I was about to bite the dust
but it turned out to be a bust
when you, my sunrise surprise,
saved me for another sunrise reprise!

Seeing Melody shake her head indicated to Les that she had read that message. So he promptly let the kite fall. Next he waved to the captain of the balloon, signaling him to depart.

Then Les marched up the hill to the cafe. Once he was in range, he shot arrow after arrow into the trunk of the trees on the spacious lawn. From each arrow hung a streamer with the following words:

> Just because I owe you my life
> you don't have to be my wife
> just take my last coupon
> and I'll be right away gone

Melody was outraged. "I'll never forgive you for this ridiculous spectacle!"

This was true, everyone on the beach was looking up at them. But Les felt no embarrassment. He felt no compulsion to hide. He felt no craving for invisibility. He recalled the words of the mustached lady, "What do you care?" After all, he was a dead man. An invincible dead man.

"So who are you today? Robin Hood?" Melody confronted him.

"It was a toss-up, between Les Dan Hood and Robin Nil. Anyway, as promised, my last Medley Brunch Cafe coupon."

She nearly ripped it as she gruffly took it from him. "Our mistake, not putting an expiration date on these."

"So now I'll take my leave," Les gave a bow. "Goodbye Melody."

"Wait a minute," she said fiercely. "I have a few things to say to you. And what do you mean by those messages?"

"Something I've been dying to tell you for almost a week."

"Which is?"

"I went to Melancholy Beach to take my life the other day. But when I saw you, I didn't want to die anymore. I wanted to live in the worst way. Or maybe I should say in the best way. The sight of you changed everything."

Melody looked at him for a long while without saying anything. She slowly crumpled the coupon and put it in her pocket. First she looked up at her customers, then to the crowd at the beach. "I hate you for putting me on the spot like this."

"I'll gladly take that hate with me to my dying day."

"Please stop with your talk of dying," she said, straining to control her temper.

"I'm sorry. I've said what I've come to say so I'll go now."

"I'm not finished," she said. "We have to talk. But this is not the time or place."

"Whenever and wherever you say."

"Tomorrow then, at Melancholy Beach. At sunrise."

"You can count on it."

"And I never want to see you again after that. Do you understand?"

30   YOU BEING YOU

On the way home, Les stopped at the Equation Beach Flower Shop and picked up a dozen lilies. The sales clerk offered to enclose a free coupon for the Medley Brunch Cafe but Les smiled and declined. He no longer needed a coupon as a pretext to see Melody.

It took a long while for him to fall asleep that night. He was filled with euphoric anticipation at the prospect of seeing Melody again. However, she had insisted it would be their last meeting. That thought filled him with gloom. So he lay restlessly between feelings of jubilation and sorrow. He listened to the sighing of the falling waves. He felt the caress of the wind carrying the fragrance of honeysuckle and jasmine. Finally he fell asleep to his own waves of sadness, waves of joy.

It was still dark when Les awoke the next morning. He walked to the nearest convenience store and called a taxi for his ride to Melancholy Beach as it was still too early for the buses.

When he arrived at the trail head, stars were beginning to fade in the sky. The courtesy sign indicated "Occupied." He assumed it was Melody's doing and continued down the winding path. When he passed through the tunnel and came out at its end, he saw her facing the sea at the water's edge, in the half light of dawn. She looked quite different, as she did each time he saw her. But she was also the same - radiant and ravishing. Even though she was already holding a dozen lilies, he sheepishly handed her the ones he brought. She thanked him and handed him a bag of pastries.

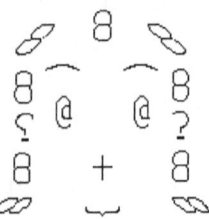

"From your last coupon," she said. "Nice of you to come without a disguise."

"Scariest thing I've done."

"It becomes you."

"What?"

"You being you."

What? All this time he was trying to be somebody else so he could be with her. And she was saying it was okay for him to be himself? All that effort he had put into hiding his ordinary self, had not been necessary at all. Les felt foolish at the ironic discovery. He was humbled into silence.

They walked along the shore line, looking at the dawn's changing light. When the sun began its rise at the line of the horizon, she stopped him to watch the first rays pierce the morning sky.

"A sunrise reprise," she said, "if I can borrow your words. It's the same sunrise every day, day after day, but it never gets old. I never get tired of it. Every time, it's like the first time, another new surprise."

"It's like that with anything you love, isn't it?"

"Some surprises are good for one time only though."

"You mean today's sunrise?"

"I told you I can't see you after today."

"I know. But anyway, I'm glad I'm here for a different reason this time than the last."

"As long as you never go back to that reason."

"What was your reason?"

She looked away to the horizon and said, "Same as yours."

"What?" Les was shocked. "How is that possible? You're so beautiful."

"What do you mean by that?"

"I don't know. I always had this thought that beautiful people led blessed lives, free from mundane troubles like the rest of us."

"Get serious. You're so juvenile. If you must know, my life is a total wreck."

"How can that be?"

"Never mind. We're not getting into that now. All I want you to know is that I don't usually go around screaming at strangers. I was just upset with you that first morning because you spoiled my plans."

"I was thankful you spoiled mine."

"In a way it was my fault because I asked for you."

"Wait, what? How?"

"I was really upset that morning for something that happened the night before. I felt I had been betrayed by fate. And the only way to show defiance was to take my life. I wanted to prove my life was in my hands, that I had freedom of will. So I dared fate to stop me, to show me a sign. And just when I was about to run headlong into the crashing waves, you appeared. I took you as the sign. You were the messenger. Showing me I wasn't in charge after all. That's why I was furious with you."

"That made you my messenger too," Les said. "It worked both ways."

"Yippeeee. Two peas in a ridiculous pod."

"I like the sound of that. Has a certain intimacy to it."

"Don't start down that road. It only leads to a dead end."

"How do you know?"

"In ways you don't know, I know."

"How?"

"It's not for you to know."

"Fine, but by now it's pretty obvious I'm crazy about you."

"And we can't let it get any crazier."

"Why not? Who's making the rules?"

"Look, I asked for this meeting so I could explain myself and apologize for my hostile behavior. Now I've done it and that's all there is to it. So thank you for coming."

She unwrapped her lilies, as well as the ones that Les gave her. Then she walked to the water's edge and tossed them into the violent waves. She remained there for a while, as if she were all alone, completely unaware of Les.

He watched the flowers being slammed to the shore by the waves, their petals torn, having no chance against the ferocity of the sea's upheaval.

When Melody returned to Les, he said, "You did that our first morning too."

"They're for my mother and . . . she's actually buried in Mexico. So the ocean here is her proxy grave site."

"How long ago did she . . . ?"

"Sometimes it feels like ages ago. Other times it feels like yesterday."

"How did she . . . "

"I'd rather not go into that."

"Sorry."

"Well, I've said what I came to say, so I'll leave now."

"Wait. We both had our reasons for coming here the other day. And those reasons are still hanging in the air."

"You can't play doctor. Not with my reasons."

"I'm not asking you to nurse my reasons either. Just let me see you again."

"We're both damaged people, Les. There's no future in it."

"I'm not asking for your future. Just today. This afternoon. Or tonight."

"No and no and no. Is that final enough?"

"All right." Les sighed and accepted her pronouncement. At least he had had another sunrise with her. He wished for thousands more, but it was not to be. This really was the end. It all seemed quite unreal. "You go ahead then. I think I'll stay here for a while."

"Good bye and good luck, Les." They shook hands.

"I'll never forget you," Les said.

"Don't talk like that. It makes me ill."

Les pursed his lips and remained silent. He kept his place and watched her walk away.

When she reached the cave, she turned around. "You're not going to do anything stupid after I leave, are you? I have enough hanging over my head. I can't be the blame-person if you . . ."

"Define stupid."

"Exactly the way you're acting now."

"It's nothing for you to be concerned about. We don't mean anything to each other, remember?"

"Now you're being childish."

"I suppose it comes from being damaged."

"You know, I actually liked you, until just now. You're a real piece of work."

"From one damaged person to another, goodbye Melody."

She glared at him, as if about to explode into a rage. "I hate you! It's not fair." She looked about her in exasperation.

Les turned his back to her, and faced the sea.

After another moment of silence, Melody called out, "Come here, you impossible man!"

Les turned around.

"You're coming with me," Melody said. "I don't trust you here alone."

"Why? What does it matter? What do you care what I do? There's nothing between us."

"Get over here now, or I swear I will hurt you."

"We've already said our goodbyes."

"I can't believe you're doing this to me. All right, all right. I'll meet you just one more time."

"When?"

"Today, after I get off work."

"Where?"

"Somewhere with people. So you can't do anything stupid. The Wonder Mile Walkway. Are you satisfied?"

"I'm thankful."

"You are so exasperating. Now, hurry up, or I'll be late. I can't have Yolanda and Esmeralda worrying about me. Where do you want me to drop you off?"

"The convenience store by the pineapple plantation will do."

"Is that where you work?"

"I don't work. So I have all day to think about you."

"Stop it. That kind of talk's not going to get you very far with me."

31   WITH YOU AS ME

In the afternoon, Les met Melody at the entrance to the Wonder Mile Walkway. She had a bag of muffins with her. They made their way to the heart of the transparent tunnel and took a seat on a bench. They watched the luminous fish among the shimmering coral and the sway of the sea grass on the sand bed.

"Just to be clear," Melody said. "You're on your own after this."

"Understood."

"You can't threaten me with a stupid stunt."

"I know I stooped pretty low this morning. I was just desperate to see you again."

She ignored his imploring tone and handed him a strawberry muffin. "Here, why don't you get busy on this." And she took out a blueberry muffin for herself.

Les took her cue and said nothing more.

They ate quietly, surrounded by the sea's brilliant swim of colors.

When they were both finished, Les continued to sit and watch the slow flowing movements of the nonchalant fish, who would occasionally speed away without warning. He recalled his first dream of drowning under the sea. The underwater world was far from threatening now.   Sitting beside Melody, that dream felt as if it had taken place in some forgotten time in someone else's past, not his.

Finally Melody said, "They're so beautiful with all their colors. I wonder what they think of us. We must look like monsters to them."

"You could ask them."

"What would you ask them?"

"Hmm . . . if they dream at night."

"I would ask if they were satisfied to be who they were."

"You mean that parrot fish might rather be a burr fish? Or that pipe fish be a stingray?"

"More like, does that starfish want to be a bigger, stronger, faster, starfish of the future? Is it tormented because it can only be the starfish of today?"

"What's wrong with wanting to be better?"

"Carried to the extreme, it's like a disease."

"Are you speaking of someone specific?" Les felt somewhat self-conscious, wondering if she knew something about his former quest to change himself.

"Never mind. Let's just get to the reason why we're here now."

"Well, I did have kind of a speech prepared but it's all jumbled up now in my mind."

"I can't un-jumble it for you."

"Okay, so here goes. The thing is . . . I've changed since I've met you. I'm doing things I never thought I would. Like that whole scenario yesterday with the Robin Hood outfit. That wasn't me. Of course, it was me. It was me and not me at the same time. Maybe more me, or less me. I don't know. But in another way, I feel more like me than ever before. The point is, it all started with you. Without you, none of this would have happened to me."

"That's a lot to put on a girl. I don't want that."

"No, I don't mean it as a burden. I'm just grateful. The past few days, each day, you were the reason I wanted to get to the next day."

"The load is definitely getting heavier."

"How can I say it any lighter?"

"I'm sorry, but I just can't be the reason you make it to tomorrow."

Les felt frustrated. "I don't mean it in an obligatory way."

"Fine. Make me the girl that got you to yesterday, and leave it at that."

"Well, what gets you to tomorrow?"

"Just plain and simple stupid habit. No, that's not right either. It wouldn't be fair to . . . I suppose, mainly, it's my mother. But sometimes she's also the reason I don't want to get to tomorrow."

Melody looked away to the tranquil underwater scene just beyond the curving pane. "At times like this I wish I were a fish."

"Do you want me to ask that angelfish to trade places with you?"

"You can't fix me, Les."

"I don't want to. I think you're perfect."

"You're making me nauseous. I have to go."

"Wait. Just one more thing. When I first saw you, I thought I had to be someone else to be with you. And it's like a miracle, to see I'm able to be with you as me. I like being me when I'm with you. That's never happened with anyone else."

"You're an absolute nightmare."

"Is there someone else?"

"What?"

"Are you already in a relationship?"

"No, god no. There's no time for that. You have no idea what's going on, Les. The mess I'm in."

"I promise I won't try to clean up your mess. Whatever it is. I probably couldn't anyway. All I want is to be with you. That's all. No fixing problems. No playing doctor. Just meet me again tomorrow. I have two free passes to The Blossom Ice Palace."

"Oh right, from your long lost adopted brother of the twice removed step cousin prematurely conceived by a bridesmaid of an annulled marriage."

"Close enough."

"Why don't you ask Yolanda or Esmeralda? They like you. They think you're perfect for me. You won them over with that Robin Hood caper."

"I can hardly handle one girl. How could I two?"

"I wish they'd take you off my hands."

"Let me take you off your hands."

"There is absolutely no reason for us to keep this going. None."

"We're two damaged peas in a pod. Your words. We don't need reasons. Reasons are poison to us."

"Then no, for no reason."

"Now you're being unreasonable."

"You're hounding me, Les. It's not pleasant."

"It's hounding by bark, not by bite."

"Doesn't help."

"You said you were in some kind of a mess. The Ice Palace will get your mind off things. A change of scenery. At least for an afternoon. And I can tell you about my nightmares."

"Whoopee do. Can't wait. As if I haven't enough nightmares of my own."

32 TO DIE ANOTHER'S DEATH

The next afternoon, they met at the entrance of the Ice Palace, winter jackets in hand. As usual Melody looked beautifully different, but also recognizably the same.

This time it was she who asked Les, "It is you, isn't it?"

"Who else would I be?" Les replied.

"I remember telling you, you being you becomes you."

"Which means I'm no longer trapped in my pre-me me. I'm free to be a different me."

"Are you trying to be like me?"

"No, only to show there's more to me than me. At least I'm not disguising myself as someone else. I'm disguised as my very own another self."

"You're enough as one, Les."

"But what about you? I love the way you're different every day. Of course you're still you. I know that. But there's more to you than you. And I love all the you-s."

Melody sighed and looked away for a moment. Then she said, "Repeat after me: this is absolutely, positively, categorically, unmistakably the last time we meet."

"Come on."

"No, say them. Say the exact words."

"I just don't understand you sometimes."

"I'm waiting."

Les dutifully repeated her words.

She added, "And neither one of us is to bear the burden of guilt for any foolish actions of the other, after we part today."

Once again Les repeated her words, without conviction. Feeling deflated, he handed their passes to the gate attendant, who let them in.

It was Saturday and the indoor park was filled with families and sunburned tourists taking a day off from the beach. The reindeer sleigh ride had the shortest line so they opted for that first. When their turn came and they settled into their sleigh, Sir Wintry's voice came over the public sound system.

"Attention guests from near and far, the Blossom Ice Palace extends a special welcome to Les Dan Nil and his lovely companion Miss Melody Utmost. Enjoy your stay!"

Completely taken by surprise, Les looked up at Sir Wintry's office window. He held a mike in one hand and waved to them with the other. They both waved back as the sleigh took off.

"So you do know him," Melody said. "You get around."

"Only lately. Because of the dreams that led me to you."

"That's right. Your nightmares. I'm all ears."

As the sleigh ride led them through the park's white winterscape, Les recounted his three dreams to Melody.

When the ride was over and they got out of the sleigh, they took a table at a cafe for tea and hot chocolate.

"They were all dreams of death," Melody said, referring to Les's nightmares.

"Sent me into a panic. I was afraid to die as me before I met you. Now I'm not. The Blue Sleep can't touch me. You helped me defeat it."

"How could you have died as someone else?"

"I was crazy, all right? All my life I couldn't stand being me, and . . ."

"You're trying to win me over by telling me you're crazy?"

"Was. Past tense. Okay? But after meeting you, everything's turned around."

"And you can't live without me."

"You just won't let me in, will you?"

"I agreed to meet you today because you promised you wouldn't bring this up. You keep making a liar out of yourself. Just like with those silly disguises. Nothing can happen between us,

Les."

"You're right, I keep singing the same old song. From now on I promise . . . "

"No, don't promise."

"All right. I'm changing my tune. How about a ride in the gondola?"

"Much better. There's hope for you, after all."

From the gondolas they went on to view the animals--seals, penguins, polar bears and so on. Then they tried ice skating, first time for both, which turned out to be a disaster. They had slightly better luck with snowboarding, after taking a brief lesson. By then they were too exhausted to go skiing. They sat on a bench and watched the others. Wisps of machine-made snow swirled slowly all around them.

"I'm having a nice time, Les."

"You have stories to tell Yolanda and Esmeralda."

"I broke their hearts when I told them this was to be our last meeting."

"You're good at that. Breaking hearts."

"Am I going to have to make you say another vow?"

"No. Absolutely, positively, categorically, unmistakably no."

"You're learning."

"You're a great teacher."

"Not good enough since it's taken me this long to get through to you."

"I wasn't this stubborn until I met you."

"So it's my fault. Haven't I been giving you all the right signals? I mean, you can't accuse me of leading you on."

"No, you've been very surgical in carving up my heart. With laser like precision."

"Just when I was getting my hopes up about you," Melody sighed. "Okay, you asked for this. Here's the final deal-breaker. It's about why I look a little different every day."

"But beautifully the same."

"Stay with me now. Have you ever seen anyone else change the way I do?"

"That's what I love about you. It makes you exciting. Each time I see you, you're someone new. But you're the same at the same time."

"It's a disorder, Les. I can't stand who I am."

"I don't have a problem with it."

"I'm serious."

"To me you're perfect."

"It's like talking to a brick wall. I'm trying to tell you why you don't want me."

"Are you kidding? You have no idea how you changed my life. I was nothing before I met you. I lived alone, hating the world, hating myself, a recluse on a beach without a name."

"Unbelievable. You're the Mad Hatter of Mad-hattan. I should have guessed when I dropped you off at the pineapple field yesterday."

"Not a very good resume, I admit, but I . . ."

"This is worse than I thought," Melody said. "Sorry Les. I'm going now. I'm ill, you're mad. A pathetic combination. Have a nice life. Goodbye." And she left him.

"But I have two coupons to the Kite And Archery Center."

She did not turn around to reply.
And just like that it was finally all over.

33   BUMBLING SINCERE

That night, up in the tree house, Les lay in his sandbox bed staring at the abundance of stars. He decided against a dramatic death. He would simply lie still, forsaking food and water, until eventually he passed away. He wondered how long it would take. Three or four days? Maybe a week? Surely not more than ten days. Probably he would lose consciousness long before that. He would die in his sleep. So the Blue Sleep would win out in the end, after all.

He wondered what kind of dream the final dream would be. One thing the Blue Sleep had not delivered yet was death by fire. So far it had covered water, wind and snow. If it was fire, would it be a forest fire? Or maybe a volcanic eruption, which would bury him under a flow of lava. What other natural catastrophes were there? Tornadoes, hurricanes, tidal waves, earthquakes. He could be struck by lightning.

But then again, why should he die in a dream of such grandiose events? He could die by a minor event like a snake bite, a jellyfish sting, or even a tree falling upon him. There were so many ways to die. And he could depend on the Blue Sleep to know all the ways. Had anyone ever taken an actual count of the different ways to die?

He wondered which dream the Blue Sleep had delivered to his grandfather on the night of his death. And with that thought, Les finally fell asleep.

Then much later, at some timeless point, he heard someone shout, "Wake up!"

He felt his body being shaken.

"Wake up."

He sat up, shocked to see Melody standing over him. It was not yet sunrise but he could see her clearly in the twilight, with a forlorn look on her face.

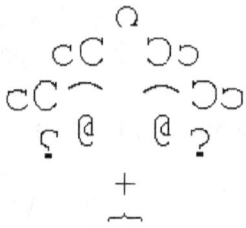

Then that look suddenly changed to one of anger. "You used me!" She screamed.

"What?"

"You used me to get to my father!"

"What are you talking about? I don't even know your father."

"Don't lie to me."

"Wait a minute." Then Les looked closely at Melody's face. "The Professor. You have his nose!"

"Don't get cute with me, you imbecile!"

"I see it now. The resemblance. No wonder you looked familiar."

"Stop playing dumb!"

"I'm sorry. I never made the connection. Besides, Sir Wintry yesterday said your last name was Utmost. But your father's last name is Sequel."

"My mother and father never officially married. When I was born I was given her last name."

"How could I have known?"

"Don't give me that. I know everything now. You were after that stupid evolution potion. And when my father said no, you decided to use me as leverage."

"No, you have it all wrong. Yes, I wanted that elixir. But only in the beginning. Because I wanted to change. But after I met you, the potion didn't matter anymore. You made it all right for me to be me."

"I don't believe you. Not with your history of lies. I feel like an idiot, falling for your coupon tactics."

Then the sunrise flushed Nameless Beach with its first light of day.

"What do you mean by 'falling?'"

"I fell for you from the start, you moron. You seemed so simple and uncomplicated. Not like everybody I knew--twisted and obsessed or scarred and wounded, including me. And your idiotic disguises, they were so inept, so transparent. You were like a bumbling child giving such earnest effort. How could I not fall for you?"

"Then why did you turn me away?"

"Because I'm sick. I'm diseased. I'm abnormal. I couldn't get you involved with me. I didn't want to ruin your life. You deserved something much better than I could give you."

"There's no one better for me than you."

"Didn't you hear me? I'm not normal!"

"So what? I'm the Mad Hatter of Mad-Hattan."

"You don't understand, I've been chemically infected. I have an incurable condition."

"I have an incurable condition too . . . you. Before I met you, I thought I wanted to be somebody. But now I understand, it's more important to be *for* somebody. I love you, Melody."

"I hate that word. It's love that ruins everything. In the name of love we do the most stupid, atrocious, diabolical things."

"For me it's just the opposite. I'm on top of the world because of love. What's so diabolical about that?"

"You just wait."

34   AS TIME STOPS BY

By then the sunrise had cleared the line of the horizon on its ascending path towards noon. The sound of songbirds throughout the forest filled the air, bearing the fragrance of honeysuckle, jasmine and mimosa. A long line of pelicans in formation flew by southwards, down the length of the beach. Sandpipers raced away from the reach of falling wavelets, their legs in a blur.

Melody's anger seemed suddenly spent. She sat down on the suspended swing, her shoulders slumped. She looked about in silence for a while. Then she said, "Quite a place you have here, Les."

"Thanks to my grandfather."

"All beaches on the island are public by law. How did he find a loophole?"

"It was a gift from a grateful nation when he won an Olympic gold medal. No one had ever even qualified for the Olympics from here before that. Or even since. He remains the one and only athlete to represent Emoticonda in Olympic history."

"Had no idea."

"Well, fame dies fast."

"Still, you must be proud."

"In a lot of ways. For one thing, he wanted the beach to remain as pure and pristine as possible, in its original state. When I was small we only came here on weekends and school holidays. We camped, staying in tents. When he died, he stipulated in his will, no construction on the grounds."

"And in other ways?"

"What do you mean?"

"There must have been a down side to him."

"I can't hold anything against him. He's the only parent I had. I don't remember my real parents at all. They both died in a boating accident when I was still in diapers. Anyway, there was one thing that my grandfather kept drilling into my head which got to be a bit much after a while. He told me over and over and over, every chance he had, 'You've got to be somebody. Or your life's worthless. Make a name for yourself. Be somebody!'"

"So you decided to be a nobody instead. Hiding out in your private paradise."

"His shoes were pretty big to fill. I just wasn't a natural athlete like he was. He tried to turn me into one. But I guess I didn't have enough of his genes."

"Genes, that's a big can of worms."

"For you?"

"Let's stick with your grandfather for now."

"Needless to say, I was a big disappointment to him."

"The real question is, are you a disappointment to yourself?"

"In this moment, with you, far from it."

"You have to take me out of the equation."

"Can't you stay in it, just for today? I can make you a grand breakfast with fresh catch from the sea."

"Well, it's my day off. And I'm starved. So, sure. Why not? Just remember there's a time limit."

While Les sat and fished from his usual

boulder, he watched Melody in the water with her white flowing dress. It didn't take long for him to get his first catch. Then a while later he got his second.

Melody finished her swim and joined him in his walk to the tree house. There she slipped out of her wet clothes and put on a clean T-shirt and swim trunks Les lent her. She hung her dress out in the sun to dry. Then they rappelled back down together, each with a small satchel slung over the shoulder.

She plucked fresh fruit from the trees while Les gathered some vegetables from the garden. They took the ladder back up. Melody swung back and forth in the swing with her eyes closed like a carefree child as Les pan-fried their fish with garlic and herbs.

Being a nobody was perfectly fine with Les for the time being. He felt as if the world were his own. He felt full, not of himself, but of life. There was no room within him for him, life took up all the spaces.

They ate breakfast at the table not saying very much. They simply took in the richness of all that was around them—the sea and sky, the beach, the forest, the songs of hidden birds in the far recesses of the trees, the intermittent breeze wafting a changing mix of floral fragrances, and the sunlight, sending its dappled streams through the overhang of leaves, warming them to the passage of their day. Sparrows pecked at the bits left in the frying pan.

They spent the rest of the day at play--zooming along the zip lines, soaking in the hot tub among the boulders, snorkeling out to the coral reef, chasing sandpipers, shooing seagulls. They also collected honey from the boxed beehives, raided the garden at lunchtime, and took a nap in the afternoon.

They had dinner that began at sunset and ended with candle light under the star-lit sky.

"It's getting late," Melody said.

"The day went so fast."

"The night is going by too."

"We can't stop time, can we?"

"That's why maybe you should ask me to stay the night before it runs out."

"Oh, I, ah . . . "

"I accept. And now will you walk with me to the pay phone at the convenience store so I can call Yolanda and Esmeralda? I can't have them worrying about me."

"It's almost like they're your mother."

"More like sisters that I never . . . never mind." She took his hand and led him away from the table.

At one point during their walk through the forest, Melody stopped him, turned off the flashlight and kissed him. For the rest of their walk, they stopped often to kiss and hold each other, each moment a timeless step into the breathless swirl of eternity.

"You know I have sink holes in my memory?" Melody said.

"What does that mean?"

"It's very strange. I'm forgetting things from my earliest times. For one thing I can't recite my A-B-C's or do-re-mi's."

"But you're talking perfectly."

"If you say the alphabet, I can repeat it right afterward. But like an hour later, I'll have forgotten it. Same thing with nursery rhymes. I can repeat them after you, but they don't stay in my memory."

"How about 'Row your boat?'"

Melody shook her head.

So Les took the lead and they sang it together in a round through the pineapple fields, until they arrived at the payphone outside the convenience store.

As Les listened to Melody speak first to Yolanda, then Esmeralda, he suddenly remembered that he was supposed to call Stu Harking. But he didn't want to turn his thoughts away from Melody. He wanted to remain under the spell of euphoria she had cast. He would call Stu another time.

For the moment, he was too enraptured by the magical turn of events. He had wanted a super evolutionary potion in order to win Melody's heart. He had had no confidence that he himself could be a worthy match to Melody. And yet, here he was, holding her in his arms without the help of any elixir. By some miracle, Melody was content to be with him as Les, with nothing added. He didn't need to be anyone else to be with her. He only had to be himself. And it was so effortless.

35   COUNTING KNACKS

Back at the tree house, Les and Melody lay together looking up at the moon and the stars beyond the screen of overlapping leaves.

"I think I like the idea of The Blue Sleep," Melody said.

"What do you mean?"

"Dying in my dreams."

"Stop it. Besides, it's just some old wives tale my grandfather passed on to me. Who knows, maybe he made it up himself."

"He sounds like a wise man to me."

"A gold medal doesn't make you perfect."

"Nothing does."

"I know my grandfather meant well when he told me to be somebody. He was trying to inspire me. To direct me to some bright future. But as a kid, not yet having accomplished anything, it just confirmed that I was worthless. Worth wasn't something you came into the world with. It was something you had to earn. And until you got it, you had no value."

"It works the other way around too, you know?"

"How?"

"You can start out with worth, and lose it later."

"Is that your story?"

"Another can of worms, Les. You have a knack for finding them."

"Okay, that knack's going out the window, right here and now. Forever. "

"I don't want you to be completely knack-less."

"Which knacks do you like?"

"Oh, let me count the ways . . ."

Later, still awake under the starlight, Melody said, "This place reminds me of my childhood."

"You lived at a nameless beach?"

"No. But I remember zipping along canopies in lots of different jungles and forests, some places so remote they didn't have names. I traveled all over the world with my mother and father. Africa, South America, Australia, the Far East, the South Pacific. Never went to school. I was home-schooled by them. They were both brilliant scientists, always on expeditions gathering serums from exotic insects and animals; seeds, roots and nectar from rare trees and plants. It was such a magical, adventurous time."

"What was it all for? What were they working on?"

"It was mainly my father's project which my mother assisted. At the time he was working on a formula to achieve a quantum leap in evolution."

"The Evolution Accelerator Solution?"

Melody paused for a moment, as if unsure whether she should go on. Then she continued with her story.

The first version of the EAS was called QLEF. It stood for Quantum Leap Evolution Formula. If it was successful with one person, my father could mass produce it for everyone. Then we'd have a world full of advanced, harmonious, kind and loving people. The day of the experiment was a big occasion. The press was kept in the dark on purpose, but there was a gallery of scientists from all over the country, and I stood next to them, watching the event through a transparent dome. My father had five graduate assistants and my mother had three graduate assistants. There were about a thousand wires and tubes attached to my father, who lay on an operating table. It was a pretty simple procedure. My mother just injected the QLEF solution with a syringe into the vein in my father's arm. He wasn't even put to sleep. What took so long was monitoring all the instrument readings. They would get a reading from one instrument, then make adjustments on five others, or get new readings from seven instruments and adjust one instrument. It went on like that for hours. It got boring pretty quickly for a ten year old. I ended up going out in the hallway to get a snack from a candy machine.

Well, to make a long story short, the experiment turned out to be a total disaster. My father couldn't even talk straight. He didn't make a single step forward in his evolution. In fact , he had degenerated. That's when people labeled his speech 'giblet gibberish.' He was ridiculed and disgraced by the scientific community, lost his funding, lost his position at the university, and so self-exiled us to Mexico. It was a dark, depressing time for us. My father was incoherent half the time. I couldn't understand his speech. Neither could my mother.

During that time, my mother poured over all

the journals, documents, instrument readings from that day to find out what went wrong. She couldn't believe it had failed and she was determined to find out the cause. My father wanted everything destroyed. He no longer wanted to work on his lifelong dream. He gave up hope.

But my mother convinced him to wait a while, and you know what, after about six months, she discovered that the dosage had been diluted by fifty percent. She had to find out how that happened. Obviously that explained the failure of the experiment.

So she started contacting all the former graduate assistants on that experiment. She grilled them one by one through letters and phone calls. But nothing turned up to explain how the dosage could have been halved. There was one graduate assistant my mother never got to question though, Lydia, because she had died from a motor scooter accident. But her ex-boyfriend, also a graduate student at the time, came to talk to my Mom in person.

He turned out to be Stu Harking. While working on his masters at the university, he had also been a competitive body-builder, dreaming of winning the Mr. Universe title. A back injury and subsequent paralysis from the waist down naturally took him out of competition. He was never too clear on the exact timing of these events. Anyway, although he couldn't provide any information on Lydia's possible mistake during the QLEF experiment, by pure coincidence, we discovered that Stu understood my father's giblet gibberish perfectly.

So naturally he proved to be indispensable as an interpreter-translator. My Mom offered him a position as an assistant to my Dad, since he claimed to be a big fan of Dad's work anyway. And Stu's been with us ever since. With better communication through Stu, my mother pressed and cajoled my father to take up the work of creating another QLEF solution but my father put his foot down and destroyed the entire archive of documents.

Eventually, after another six months of my father withering away doing nothing, my mother threatened to leave him if he didn't snap out of it and get back to what he did best. So Dad came up with a new theory, and a new approach to "save" emoticon-kind. That meant we had to start traveling again, to collect all the exotic nectar, extracts, pollens, seeds and oils.

To raise funds for those trips my mother used her knowledge of herbs and spices to make unbelievable tortillas, sopapillas, and taco shells. In no time at all she had a thriving business selling these whole-sale. That's how we met Pedro and Magdalena, who stayed behind to run the business with their relatives, while we went globetrotting. Yolanda and Esmeralda came with me to keep me company. It was such an incredible time. I was sure I was the happiest person in the world.

It was so good to see my father back to doing what he loved, with a fresh approach.

36 BYPASSED CHILDHOOD

His new tactic was to forget about leap-frogging evolution. Instead he decided to by-pass childhood. His theory was that emoticons spent too much time in childhood. There were certain animals in nature that achieved instant adulthood the minute they're born. So they have immediate coping mechanisms to deal with life on a mature, fully functional, capable basis, whereas emoticons spend eighteen or twenty years before they reach maturity.

That means they deal with life as immature, dysfunctional, incapable creatures for eighteen or more years, accumulating layers and layers of misconceptions, mistakes, and misunderstandings, so that by the time they reach adulthood, they're misguided, malformed, and misinformed, full of crippling, corrupting, contemptible unresolved issues. Then they spend most of adulthood trying to overcome their childhood wounds and injuries, which they also inflict on others by their own ignorance. Is it any wonder the world is full of thievery, treachery, cruelty, murder and wars?

My father wanted to eradicate all that. By eliminating childhood, emoticons could handle life in a pure unspoiled state of mind and body with wisdom and intelligence. His answer was to create MABE, the Mature At Birth Extract.

And the solution had to be administered at the time of conception. Initially my father was toying with the idea of finding a virginal surrogate mother who would be willing to accept artificial insemination. But once they considered all the legal ramification that might arise if the experiment failed, my father put the project on hold.

During that self-imposed break, my father once again became despondent and discouraged. Before he succumbed to full blown depression, my mother offered herself as the experimental subject. And if the experiment succeeded, I would have a brother or a sister. I was excited about that.

And so my mother began taking daily dosages of the MABE solution from day one. Each dosage was specific to each successive day so if you took one dosage either before or after the designated day, it would break down the entire sequential stream, which was crucial to the success of the experiment. Then as time went on, a sonogram revealed my mother was having twin girls. I was thrilled. Two sisters at once!

But my father became frantic. He was worried because the dosages were designed for one infant, not two. Not only would that dilute the effectiveness of the solution by fifty percent for each, but different effects were going to each so that the other was not getting those particular effects at all. So you were going to end up with unbalanced infants. And doubling the dosage wasn't possible because no reserves had been created.

So my father's experiment seemed like a failure even before it had the chance to see the light of day. He wanted to abort the experiment, but my mother convinced him to show faith. She believed that even if the experiment failed and the two arrived into the *world with birth defects, they still deserved to live, and that they would be given all the love and care that any normal child would get. Though my father tried to convince her otherwise, my mother remained firm in her resolve, persuading my father to make the adjustments as best he could and put his trust in fate.*

Another unrelated event that took place during that time of my mother's pregnancy, was the change that came over Stu. His body became more effeminate. All his upper body builder muscles shrunk, he lost his facial hair, and his skin became soft and girlish. First he blamed it all on the water, then some pollen, then the hot climate, but we never found out exactly what caused it. We were sad for him but we were too excited about the pending arrival of my sisters to make his troubles a priority.

So a home-birthing was arranged with a mid-wife to assist my mother. For good luck, we had extra lilies all over the house. We also had a taxi on stand-by, in case my mother had to be rushed to the hospital. Of course I was there, with Yolanda and Esmeralda and their mother, Magdalena. It was supposed to be a happy joyous occasion. The arrival of two new beings into the world. But it was horrible, Les. It was the most abominable thing I'd ever witnessed.

I love my father, Les. He's not evil. His intentions are good. He's an idealist. He has a wonderful heart. But the results he produces, they're the work of the devil. What I saw was diabolical. There's no other way to put it. It's just so sad that in trying to do good, he ends up committing atrocities.

My sisters, they were supposed to be born as adults, but adults in miniature. They were programmed to maintain their infant size until the birthing was complete. My mother's contractions somehow set off a growth spurt in them and they began to grow in size during the birthing, blocking their own delivery through the birth canal, and swelling my mother's stomach to ghastly proportions. My father began to perform a caesarean but as he was completing the initial incision, the twins literally tore my mother apart with their powerful, fully muscular arms and legs and sharp firm fingernails and toenails. They were kicking in wild desperation themselves because not only were the umbilical cords wrapped around their necks, they had been sucking on long strands of their own fully grown hair and they were choking to death when they emerged from my mother's ripped abdomen. There was blood everywhere and of course neither the twins nor my mother survived.

The twins were almost three feet tall, laid out full length. They had adult facial features, like midgets. But they were beautifully child-like too, with baby soft skin. I never got to see their eyes.

The authorities threatened to persecute my father for infanticide and the rest of us as accomplices. It didn't come to that, but we were banished nevertheless by the community and that's when we came to Emoticonda, to somehow start anew. It was so hard to leave my mother's grave and those of my sisters.

Before we left, my father destroyed all records

of the MABE solution. He made a decision to give up his pursuit of creating better emoticon beings.

37   CLOSET PLACE

By the time Melody ended her story, the sky was the color of lavender. And the sound of songs within the forest signaled the world was already awake. Soon the sky paled, awaiting the rising of the sun.

Melody went down to refresh herself in the sea. When she returned, she had recomposed herself with a new look.

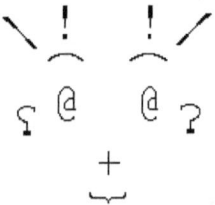

"I have some new girls to train today at the Cafe," Melody said. "In fact, I'll be busy training them all week."

"Are you telling me you won't have time to see me?"

"I'm telling you to run, now that you know all the heavy baggage I'm carrying."

"Not a chance."

"You don't get to choose."

"What are you talking about? Where is this coming from? We just had an incredible time together. The best of my life. And you weren't exactly complaining."

"I felt I owed you at least one good day."

Just then the sunlight broke through the dawn.

"No. I'm not going to be a charity case," Les insisted. "How dare you? You're not going to end this after one day. There are lots of great days left in us."

"Sorry, but the Cafe is off limits to you, as of now. And I'm never coming back here. So that's it."

"I don't get it. We're great together. You must see that. We're just getting started."

"Game over, Les. I told you there was a time limit."

"Wait a minute, who are these new girls anyway?"

"From high school. There's a split shift for the students because of the overcrowding. Freshmen and sophomores go in the morning, the juniors and seniors in the afternoon. So we're taking advantage of that situation and getting part time girls to cover two shifts."

"What for?"

"What do you mean, what for?"

"It's not like business is suddenly booming, is it? It's not Spring Break and it's not the summer high season. Why do you need more workers? Are you firing Yolanda and Esmeralda?"

"No, they're actually going to take my place."

"So that's it. You're going off somewhere?"

"Look, I already told you my sordid life story. There's nothing more to tell, all right?"

"What are you going to do once you stop

working?"

"I don't owe you any explanations."

"Yes, you do. If you're going to break up with me, you have to tell me why."

"This is not a break up. There was not enough between us for this to be a break up."

"Fine. You can't face the truth, too bad. I still want to know why you're ending this?"

"Because you're a pain in the neck. Is that good enough?"

"No, I want to know what's going on with you, how you got your disorder, how you got infected in the first place, with what? You've given me your father's story, your mother's story. But you haven't given me your whole story."

"I don't have time for this. And I don't have time for you."

She got up and put on her dress. "I have to go now. So once again, for once and for all, goodbye Les."

She rappelled down to the ground.

As she stormed off, Les called out after her. "I'm coming to the Cafe. I'm getting to the bottom of this. I'm talking to Yolanda and Esmeralda. I'm going to talk to your father."

Melody turned around violently. "Don't you dare!"

"Why? More potions in the closet?"

"You belong in the closet! This whole place is your closet. So you just stay put and shut in. You can't handle what's out there!"

Then she hurried down the path, disappearing into the woods.

38 DUMBFOUNDED

Les quickly cleaned himself up and took a taxi to Equation Beach. When he arrived at the bakery he went to the back where Tip Top was loading up a van, with the help of Pedro.

"I'm here about Melody," Les said.

"She's out front," Tip Top replied. "In the Cafe."

"No, she won't see me. I need to talk to you."

"I've got to make my run to the Ice Palace."

"I'll come with you."

"The insurance won't cover you as a non-employee if we have an accident."

"Don't worry. If I die, you'll probably be doing me a favor."

"Your life."

As they pulled out of the loading dock, Les asked Tip Top "Do you know about Melody's condition?"

"Can't keep a thing like that secret."

"Well, how did it happen? I mean, she didn't just wake up one morning with the disorder?"

"I'm not sure if I should be telling you this."

"You know I'm in love with her. I wouldn't use the information to hurt her. I just want to know, for my sake. That's all."

They made their way past the winding streets and onto the coastal highway and headed for the Ice Palace.

"It had to do with a precursor to the Evolution

Accelerator Solution, called the Childhood Memory Eraser or CME for short. The Professor theorized that most of our adult problems stem from unresolved childhood issues. So if he could eliminate childhood memories, those issues would instantly disappear, and adults would lead happier, more productive, capable lives, free from the crippling effects carried over from childhood and adolescence. When I came on board at the bakery, the Professor had given up on his research and experimentation. I think it had to do with the death of his wife. I don't know anything about that because it happened before they arrived at Emoticonda. Anyway, it was Stu Harking that helped get the Professor back on his feet. Stu reawakened the Professor's motivation. So they worked together on the CME for years. But when the work was done, the Professor suddenly got cold feet. The idea of actually using the CME on a live subject appalled him. He couldn't go through with it. He didn't want to ruin any emoticon's life if the experiment failed. Well believe it or not, Stu Harking and Melody got together and went ahead with the experiment in secret. I was dumbfounded. Don't ask me how they got paired up because Melody couldn't stand Stu. I guess her motivation was to show support for her father. Anyway, the experiment turned out to be a big failure. Of course the Professor found out. He destroyed all the records and data on the CME and vowed he would never pursue this line of research again. The side effect of the experiment is that there are holes in Melody's memory."

"She told me about that. She can't remember her do-re-mi's."

"She can't do simple addition or subtraction either. That's why she can't work the cash register at the Cafe anymore. And it's just going to get worse. I think eventually, by the time she's retirement age, she's going to be a vegetable."

"But remember the morning I came to see you here? Did anything different happen the night before?"

"I don't know. I'm not here at night."

"But did anyone mention anything out of the ordinary that happened the night before?"

"Well, now that I think about it, Magdalena and the girls, Yolanda and Esmeralda, all three were a little puffy eyed as if they'd been crying all night. The Professor might have been more quiet than usual. But Stu seemed pretty up. Good thing because his downs can get pretty intense. You don't want to be around him then. Actually, I don't want to be around him anytime. Anyway, overall, it was business as usual that morning."

"Something happened the night before, I know it."

"What?"

"I don't know, but something. A trigger event. Because the next morning when I met Melody for the first time at Melancholy Beach, she was going to . . . Never mind. Drop me off."

"Here?"

"I'll take the bus back."

Tip Top pulled over to the side of the highway. "By the way, this is slightly off topic, but something peculiar is happening to Stu Harking."

"How so?"

"He's starting to get holes in his memory, like Melody."

39   VOIDED INTO THE VOID

When Les got back to the bakery, the loading dock was locked down. He saw Yolanda and Esmeralda peeking around the corner. He walked up to them as they were putting out their cigarettes.

"Oh, please, don't tell Mama and Papa," they pleaded in unison. Yolanda put their extinguished stubs into a plastic bag and sealed it. Esmeralda took out an atomizer and sprayed both of them with perfume. Yolanda popped a breath mint into her mouth, gave one to Esmeralda. Then she offered one to Les.

He declined and asked, "Remember the day you first saw me here at the Cafe?"

"Si, si."

"What happened here the night before?"

"What you mean?" Yolanda asked.

"Something happened to Melody that night."

"Oh, dios mio." Then the sisters exchanged looks with one another.

"I have to know. It's important."

The sisters remained silent.

"Or I'm going to your mother and father about your smoking."

"Ay, por favor, no."

"Then tell me."

Yolanda's eyes filled with tears and she turned to Esmeralda. "You say to him."

Esmeralda too, wiped her eyes. She took out her breath mint and tossed it away. Then she wiped her wet fingers on her apron and kept her head bowed. "Melody, she dying."

"What?"

"Some years ago, there was bad experiment."

"It was called CME juice, I think," Yolanda interjected.

"It make Melody sick," Yolanda continued. "So El Professor spend many years to make antidote. And last week, same night before she meet you, he give her the antidote. But it was big mistake. It make sickness go faster, not slow down. So now, Melody dying."

"No," Les countered. "No way. She's not going to die." The news gave him a strange sensation of disintegration, as if the structure of reality were crumbling, and his own persona was being voided into some formless floating void.

"El Professor say maybe two, three months."

"No, she can't die. She just can't."

"Maximum, six months," Yolanda added.

"I'm not going to stand for this."

"I'm so sorry," Yolanda said.

"Something's got to be done. I have to find a way."

"We must go now," Esmeralda said. "Our break finished."

"I have to talk to somebody."

"Please don't say to Melody, we say you this," Yolanda pleaded.

"I have to talk to the Professor."

"No, please. Or Melody find out we talk to you."

"It's her life we're talking about. You're her

friends, aren't you?"

"Si, si. Like sisters, all three."

"And you want to save her life, don't you?"

"But El Professor, he say not possible."

"No, there has to be a way. And I'm going to find the way. That's why I have to talk to him. You girls have to let me in. You have the keys, right?"

"Si, pero no."

"I can't go through the Cafe or Melody will stop me. I have to get in through the back. You have to help me."

"O, dios mio."

"You want her to live, don't you?"

"Of course, we love her very much. All our life, we love her."

"Then get me in, now."

40   ON THE VERGE OF DANGEROUS

As soon as Les was let in, he rushed to Stu's office and barged in without knocking. "I need to see the Professor!"

"Why didn't you call me?"

"I'm sorry. But Melody is dying. I have to talk to the Professor."

"And I'm the one who has the power help her, not him."

"What do you mean?"

"I told you, the Professor gave up on his EAS. But I took over his research without his knowledge."

"That's dishonest. You're a thief!"

"On the contrary, it's the act of a superior mind superseding the failures of an inferior mind."

"You think you're better than the Professor?"

"I know I am and you shouldn't question it if you want to save Melody."

"How?"

"It's quid pro quo as any arrangement in life. You do something for me and I do something for you."

"We're talking about Melody's life. You don't negotiate something like that. It's too dangerous."

"Believe me, we both want the same thing."

"Prove it."

"My very own second generation Evolution Accelerator Solution."

"What about it?"

"It's complete."

"So there was another potion. That's the answer. That's what's going to save Melody."

"We can't give this EAS directly to Melody."

"Why not?"

"Because it's not an antidote for her disorder. It's a potion to specifically create a supreme, superior emoticon of advanced intelligence."

"And that super emoticon can find the cure for Melody right?"

"Without doubt."

"What are you waiting for?"

"A subject."

"I'm here. I'm ready. By the way, was my blood okay?"

"In optimal condition."

"Then let's get on with it."

"Not so fast. The procedure has to be carried out under stringent conditions. There's extensive preparation involved."

"How long?"

"Your residence is at Nameless Beach, correct?'"

"Yes."

"Perfect. That's where the experiment will take place."

"But don't you need all those instruments in the lab?"

"We'll have to get duplicates. I'll work on that. What I need you to do is set everything up."

"Whatever you say."

"You are quite aware that everything we do from now on must be conducted in absolute secrecy."

"Can't I tell Melody I'm working on a cure for her? To give her hope?"

"Absolutely not. Remember, there is no guarantee of success with the experiment. She was the unfortunate subject of a prior experiment herself."

"I know, the CME."

"Exactly. And look how that backfired. We can't have that happening again. I won't stand for it. I can't take another failure. It'll kill me."

41 KNOW HOW

When Stu found out that Les lived in a tree house without electricity, he went into a rage. "What are you doing, you ape, living in the Stone Age? Now you just doubled all the work. Can't believe it. I'm working with a monkey."

Les bit his lip, keeping in mind the ultimate goal was to save Melody. He was willing to suffer any insults from Stu to achieve the desired result. He reminded himself that after meeting Melody, most of his debilitating self-talk had ceased. So the insults of others were a minor discomfort compared to his own former verbal self-abuse.

"Sorry," Stu said. "I keep forgetting you're not at my level in intelligence. But look, I'm still counting on you, right? Haven't got anyone else. So I'm stuck with you."

It was a busy week. Les called Stu twice a day from the payphone at the convenience store, and followed the instructions that were given him. He had solar panels set up all over Nameless Beach. Although the installers did the main work, Les assisted in laying out a redundant network of charge controllers, batteries and inverters leading to the wooden deck.

Then he hired migrant workers from the pineapple field to help him build a shanty over the deck. Since it required no foundation, and the structure was only temporary, Les considered it not a breach of his grandfather's edict forbidding

171

construction on the beach. Then he set up outlets for the various electrical monitors and measuring instruments which arrived daily at the post office. He picked them up in a truck that he had rented for the week.

Les thought of Melody from morning to night but the busy work also kept him from wallowing in pity. It was good to expend all that energy on physical work. He wished he could reveal to her all the work that was going on for her sake, but that day would come soon enough. He had to have patience.

At week's end, when he finally had time to fully realize his exhaustion, he had two surprise visitors after dinner. They were Yolanda and Esmeralda.

They looked up at him in his tree house.

"You have TV?" Yolanda asked.

"No, why?"

"You have a refrigerator?" Esmeralda asked.

"No need for it."

"Washer and dryer?" Yolanda asked.

"You want to wash clothes?" Les asked.

"No, don't be funny," Esmeralda said. "Then why you make so much electricity here?"

"Oh, that." Les remembered Stu's demand for secrecy. It would not do for the girls to find out about their plan. Referring to the solar panels, he explained, "I got tired of the dark at night."

"It looks nice up there," Yolanda said.

"Nice everywhere here," Esmeralda said. "A garden, all the trees with fruit. Even avocados."

"You're welcome to come up," Les said. "Use

the ladder. Easier than the rope."

The girls climbed up. Yolanda took a seat on a large branch and Esmeralda sat on a swing.

"Today, last day for Melody at cafe," Yolanda said.

"Now she have nothing to do," Esmeralda added. "All day she free."

"You must spend time with her," Yolanda said.

"I'd love to," Les responded. He kept in mind his secret pact with Stu. "But she hates me. She won't let me come near her."

"That's not true," Yolanda said.

"She like you very much," Esmeralda said.

"Why can't she tell me that herself?"

"Because you funny man," Esmeralda said. "You don't know nothing about how girls think."

"No argument there."

"You must make nice time with her," Yolanda said.

"We already told you she gonna die," Esmeralda reminded him.

"I don't want to hear that," Les said. "She's not dying. Not if I have anything to do with it."

"You not God. Nobody God. You can't stop God. Don't be funny, funny man," Esmeralda said.

"We ask you," Yolanda said, "Give her nice time before she die."

"I'd love to do that for her. But she won't let me in. If I go to her now, she'll probably shoot me on sight."

"No, she no shoot you. We gonna shoot you if you don't make nice time for her."

"That's right," Yolanda said. "So don't be

stupid. You love her, yes?"

"With all my heart."

"Then you must go to her."

"How?"

"Are you loco? You are the man. We no tell you how. You must know how. Not us."

"Okay, so do I call her? Or do I just show up at the bakery and . . . "

"Aye yai yai!" Esmeralda slapped herself on the forehead. "Dios mio. You crazy-funny man. Love tell you what to do. Love show you. Okay?"

Les nodded in embarrassment. "Got it."

Yolanda stood up. "Okay, now we want take some avocados for our mother, okay? She can make guacamole."

"Just one thing, don't tell Melody about the solar panels, the electricity."

"Why?"

"Because . . . well, at least not yet. When the time is right, I will tell her about them myself. All right?"

"You make nice surprise for her?"

"The best surprise of her life."

"Okay, then. We no say nothing."

42   DAY OF VALIDITY

The next morning Les went to Medley's Brunch Cafe with some more avocados. Yolanda and Esmeralda were working with four other high school girls. They thanked him for the avocados and told him Melody was sunbathing down at Equation Beach.

It did not take him long to find her. She sat in the shade of an umbrella, in a recliner, wearing a swimsuit and a white sheer long sleeve shirt. .

"I have two coupons," Les said.

"You're at the wrong place if you want muffins."

"They're for the Hurricane Beach Kite and Archery Club."

"You're still at the wrong place."

"It feels pretty right to me. It always does, around you."

"It's been an exhausting week. Can't you just let me be?"

"Why can't we be friends? For the time we

have left together . . . "

"There is no we time. You have your time. I have mine. And never the twain shall meet."

"If I were in your shoes, wouldn't you do the same for me?"

"What? Harass you with coupons?"

"You know, they were smart enough to put an expiration date on these. Tomorrow's the last day of validity."

"Oh, gee, how will I sleep tonight?"

"Listen, I know you think you're doing this for me. That by keeping your guard up you're saving me from suffering in the future. But after you're gone, and you had a chance to look back, wouldn't you feel better about yourself, knowing you let me in, and gave me what no one else could give me?"

"How did you find out?"

"I just put two and two together . . ."

"No, someone told you."

"Does it really matter who told me? What matters is I want to be with you."

"I knew Esmeralda and Yolanda couldn't keep their mouths shut."

"Forget about them for a second. I'm talking about us."

"I don't want your pity."

"And you call me exasperating. What can I do to get through to you?"

"Give up."

"Like you?"

"There's so little time, it's pointless."

"For me, one day with you, is a lifetime in the bank."

"I'm not going to be Miss Sunshine you know."

"You can be Miss Cloudy."

"My body is deteriorating, fast. It's not going to be pretty."

"You can be Miss Ugly."

"Soon I'll need a wheelchair, then I'll be bed ridden, tubes stuck in me, looking like a voodoo doll."

"Okay, Miss Voodoo. Let's just focus on today."

"I just want you to be clear about what you're getting yourself into."

"I know. Down the rabbit hole of love."

"I haven't said love yet."

"All right, we'll call it nameless. Like my beach."

"I nameless you. I suppose that works."

"And Hurricane Beach?"

Melody sighed. "Fine. Tomorrow. Only because I have nothing to do."

"And the rest of today?"

"This is it."

"Then I'll go shop for a pair of swim trunks. Be right back."

43   BY YOUR BOTH SIDES

In addition to the swim trunks and a beach towel, Les went to another store and picked up a pair of dress pants, a dress shirt and blazer. At a third store, he bought a pair of dress shoes. Then he returned to the beach and joined Melody. They spent the rest of the afternoon, sunning, swimming, and getting massages. At the end of the day, they sat together, Melody in Les's arms, looking out to sea where the sun was about to meet the horizon.

"That's one thing you don't get at my place," Les said.

"What?"

"The sunset."

"The sunrise is a nice trade off."

"Well, you do get the sunset if you climb up to the top of the boulders."

"That's how I think of you, you know."

"A boulder?"

She slapped him on his thigh. "A sunrise. It's the same sun, over the same sea, but the sameness never gets old. Every morning, a newborn sight. I see you the same way. Even with all your failed disguises, you're the same simple Les. Dependable as the next day's sunrise reprise."

"For me, it's the opposite. I love how you look different every day. Even though you're the same you. It's like seeing a new pattern of stars every night. They're the same stars, but they're arranged differently, so you're constantly seeing new constellations."

"That kind of sky wouldn't work for sailors, would it? They'd be lost every night."

"It works for a tree house dweller."

"I wouldn't mind being there now."

"Tonight you deserve a better place."

"There's no other place like your place."

"We'll find one."

"I'm getting suspicious now. You're trying to keep me away from your tree house."

"I just want to give you a special treat."

"Nameless Beach is the most special place I know."

"No. You need a change. Just for tonight."

"Hmm, you're hiding something from me."

"Fine, let's just say I've been remodeling."

"When do I get to see it?"

"Soon, it's not done yet."

"Why were you so secretive? I was starting to imagine all kinds of dark thoughts."

"Tell me one of those dark thoughts."

"No, I don't want to poison you with my darkness."

"What are you talking about? All I see in you, is everything bright and shining."

"I've heard those words before."

"I'm sure you've had lots of suitors."

"Let me see, the three most recent ones were One-Eyed Les, Sir Lesheart and Les Dan Hood aka Robin Nil."

"Did any of them fall into the dark category?"

The sun had set and it's after light still glowed faintly over the horizon.

"By my standards of darkness, didn't even come close." Melody sighed. "All right, you have the right to know who you're falling for. So here goes. It's probably the sickest thing I've ever done. And I'll carry that regret all the way to my grave. And if you want nothing to do with me after I tell you, it'll just be par for the course." She took a deep breath, let it out as she looked out to sea, then quietly said, "I let Stu Harking take me once."

Les was crestfallen. This he definitely did not expect. "He's so much older than you. And so different. I just don't get it."

"It was my bargaining chip so that he would let me take the Childhood Memory Eraser potion. I wanted to do something for my father, to lift up his spirits, to boost his morale, because he was so depressed during that period after my mother's death, and my twin sisters. I couldn't do anything to turn things around for him and it made me feel like a failure. The only thing I could think of was to take the CME to prove I believed in him and his work and that he was still a great man and should be proud of himself. I had to do it in secret because he would never have allowed it. So I went through Stu. And of course he wanted something in return. I always knew Stu was a creep. I tolerated him because my father was so dependent on him. But I generally stayed as far away from him as I could. But when push came to shove, and I had to have that CME procedure, I couldn't refuse Stu. It was a nightmare. Thank God it didn't last long but it felt like forever at the time. Anyway, if you want to leave me now, it would be a relief."

"I expected you to have had past lovers. But I never thought one of them would be Stu."

"He wasn't a lover, for God's sake. I get sick to my stomach just thinking about it. And the worst part was that he told me he loved me. That he had loved me for years. That he had watched me grow up, waiting for the day when he could claim me as his princess, blah, blah, blah. That's when I made my run to the toilet to vomit."

"That's why you can't stand words of love. "

"If I had my way, I'd kill him. I really believe I'm capable of murder when it comes to him."

"I'm sorry he hurt you."

"I had to tell you. I wanted you to know who I really was. I didn't want you to fall for me thinking I was Miss Sunshine."

"I already knew you were Miss Cloudy."

"Miss Voodoo. I'm your worst nightmare, Les."

"No, you saved me from my own nightmares. And you did what you did with Stu because you loved your father and wanted to save him. That's the bright side of your dark decision. So you can't scare me away. I'm here and I'm staying by your both sides, bright and dark."

By now the stars were appearing in the night sky.

44   MISTER, MASTER, EMPEROR

They left the beach and walked up the hill to Melody's bakery-cafe-home. As she was changing in her room upstairs, Les changed downstairs in the men's room of the cafe. Then he went back out and sat on the steps, looking out beyond the trees to the beach below and the open darkness of the sea.

From one of the upstairs windows he could hear Yolanda and Esmeralda singing a song in Spanish. It had a melody both sweet and melancholy at the same time. Then he heard the approaching sound of Stu Harking's electric power chair behind him.

In the light of Melody's revelations, Les was repulsed by Stu's presence. But they were partners to save Melody and until that went through, Les had to be civil with him.

"Day after tomorrow," Stu said.

"Everything's set," Les said.

"I'll arrive in the morning, early."

"I always get up at sunrise."

"No sunrise will ever be the same for you afterward."

"I'm looking forward to it."

"It can't come soon enough. The world order is about to change. A fearsome figure of glory will appear to take this new age by storm: a virtual Mr. World, far greater than Mr. Olympia of mere muscular fame - a truly magnificent, transcendent, ultimate, mega-galactic Mr. Universe. No, Master

Universe. Emperor Universe!"

"Thanks for the buildup, but my ambitions aren't so grand."

"Of course not. You have no great vision as I do."

"I only want to save Melody's life."

"Yes, yes, of course. A trifling matter compared to . . ."

"Melody's life, a trifle?"

"There are far more . . ."

"She's dying, even now, right this minute. I can't let that go on. I have to find a cure. That's all I care about. That's the only reason I'm doing this."

"Calm yourself young fellow, you will do all that you're able. And I shall do all that I'm able. I promise you that."

Les looked past Stu's shoulder. "Melody is coming."

"So you two are having an evening together?"

"A dinner out. Whatever I can do to ease her mind in any small way . . ."

"Day after tomorrow she will be free from her current station."

"Let's hope so."

Then Melody came up to them with an arm full of lilies wrapped in wax paper. She spoke to Les, without acknowledging Stu, "I'm famished, aren't you?"

"What do you have in mind?" Les asked. "French, Italian, Sushi?"

"Let's check into the hotel first."

Les realized Melody's comment was meant to

irk Stu. "Have a nice evening, Stu," Les said.
Stu simply glared back in silence.

45   SLIGHTING MOTHER GOOSE

They drove in Melody's car and checked into a penthouse suite in a five star hotel on a hillside high above Dancing Stars Beach. Melody set the lilies throughout their rooms. They had a candle light dinner at a ridge top restaurant that gave a view of the sea on both sides of the island. Afterward they went back to their hotel room. There they carried the double bed mattress out onto the veranda and lay under the stars.

After a long while under the spell of the night sky's silence, Melody said, "Whenever I felt sorry for myself, my mother used to remind me that even the earth got knocked around when it was young, tilting it into a lopsided spin."

"That explains why my life is so askew. Now I understand it's supposed to be out of kilter, to align with the earth's rotation."

"Some of us are more askew than others."

"Askew feels perfect right now."

"I have trouble with good times. Bad times seem more real."

Les held her face with his hands and gave her a long and timeless kiss. "Did that feel real?"

"Try me again, you lopsided fool."

After the lovemaking, Melody said, "Besides my A-B-C's being gone, another thing I don't remember is the multiplication table."

"I'm glad you're off the cash register. I get more time with you."

"Would you recite it?"

"Are you serious?"

"I'd love to hear it as I fall asleep."

"You're slighting Mother Goose."

"Start with two."

And so Les softly murmured the numbers, "Two times one is two, two times two is four, two times three is six, two times four is eight . . ."

In the morning the first thing Melody said to Les was, "Coupon time."

"Hurricane Beach, it is."

They had a champagne breakfast in their room, then took the coastal highway to the Kite and Archery Center. They were given a quick lesson on flying a kite and then were left on their own. They maneuvered a kite together, Melody within Les's arms. The wind was so strong, it dragged them along the sand. At one point their legs tangled and they fell down over each other.

"I love the feel of the wind," Melody said. "It feels like it's wiping everything away, house-cleaning the past."

"Archery lesson next. We'll blast the past with arrows."

"Can we blast the future too?"

"The future doesn't need to be blasted."

"No?"

"What would we have left if we did?"

"Now. All I want is now. To stay in now. With you. Like this. Forever now."

They kissed within the roar of the wind and the ripping sound of other kites down the beach. It was as if the world all around them were being shredded, and they were the only two safe and sound in the shelter of their embrace, fiercely defiant against the sweep of time.

The archery lesson was given at the indoor range. After a brief how-to demonstration, they practiced on their own, each with a different bow, as other archers sent arrows flying down their respective lanes.

"No showing off now, Les Dan Hood," Melody said.

"Remember to be the target," Les said. "That was Tip Top's advice."

"I know all about being a target."

"Don't we all. The trick is to tilt it to our favor. So we get the advantage."

"Align with the earth's rotation?"

"Better than the way Tip Top put it. He made it sound like suicide."

"We're both failures in that department."

"We should be proud of being failures."

"Isn't that like scraping the bottom of the barrel? What else can we be proud of?"

"That this seems to be working? Between you and me?"

Melody put her bow and arrow down. "That you didn't give up on us."

"We both took a few slings and arrows, didn't we?"

"Come here my Robin Nil," Melody said, pulling him towards her. Then she kissed him, holding him fiercely as if to seize time itself.

46 SEPARATING TIME

They returned to the hotel for the night. In the morning they awoke early, while the stars were still full in the sky. Melody gathered some lilies from the room and they checked out of the hotel.

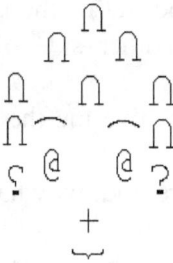

She dropped Les off on her way to Melancholy Beach for her usual sunrise greeting and the casting of the flowers to the sea in memory of her mother and sisters.

Les arrived at Nameless Beach by the light of dawn. Stu Harking was already there in his all-terrain power chair.

"You're early," Les said.

"There's no time to waste."

They went into the newly constructed "lab" building over the wooden deck. All the electrical instruments had already been turned on.

"Where's the EAS?" Les asked.

"In the refrigerator. Now lie down on the bed."

Les did as he was told. And Stu promptly set locks on Les's wrists, arms, feet and legs so that Les could not move them. His waist, chest and head were also strapped down to prevent any movement.

"Am I going to have a violent reaction?" Les asked.

"These restraints are just a precaution."

Stu stuck a needle into the vein in Les's arm and began to draw blood through a tube that passed into a cubed graduate attached to a monitoring instrument that gave a digital read out of the blood flow. Another tube led out the other side of the machine.

"I thought you were going to give me the EAS potion, not take my blood."

"Don't question my procedure. I know what I'm doing."

"But why are you taking my blood again?"

"Are you a scientist?"

"No."

"Have you performed this kind of experiment before?"

"No."

"That's right. You know nothing about it. I do. So let me do my work."

"I'd just like an explanation as to . . . "

"You simple minded fool. Just shut up or you'll ruin everything."

Les was upset, but he decided to do as he was told. There was nothing else he could do anyway. He was strapped in, like a trapped animal. And the procedure had started. He had to see it through to the end. He tried to focus on the image of himself as a new highly evolved emoticon. Ironically enough, he felt a certain melancholy for having to give up his current identity. Ever since Melody had come into his life, he had come to accept himself more and more. And there was a part of him now that wanted to hold on to his current version of Les, the one that Melody loved.

And would Melody continue to love the new Les? Would there be enough sameness in him that she could love? Or would he become completely different so that she could no longer love him? Or as a new being, would he forget all memory of his past life, including his love for Melody? Would the new Les have the heart to recognize Melody as his one true beloved? Les was starting to panic.

No. He had to focus on the purpose of this experiment. It was to save Melody's life. Even if she could no longer love him as a newly transformed being, the greater good would be served by his saving her life. And as an advanced being he would find the cure. He had to put his personal fears aside and concentrate on the health and wellness of Melody.

In the meantime Stu also began to draw his own blood into a large plastic bag.

"What are you doing?" Les asked.

"I told you not to ask questions."

"I have the right to know what's going on."

Stu remained silent and then attached the tube from the digital read out machine into his other arm.

Les realized his blood was flowing into Stu's body while Stu's blood was being drained out.

"You'd better explain yourself," Les demanded.

"Something's not right." He struggled in anger to free himself, but in vain.

Stu quietly adjusted his power chair into the reclining position. "Did you really think I'd waste the greatest creation in the history of the entire world on a nobody like you?"

Les felt the skin on the back of his neck crawl. "You're taking the EAS!"

"How astute of you at this late hour in your life."

"I knew you couldn't be trusted."

"You know how much I suffered watching you, a completely inept simpleton, win Melody's heart? I'm the one who has loved her longer than anyone. I'm the one who deserves her. And she's going to be mine, I promise you. Once I save her, she'll owe her life to me. She'll be so full of gratitude, she won't be able to deny me her love."

"That's not love, that's extortion."

"You are so small-minded. Unlike you, I have a great vision. Although not all of my visions were realized, I came to understand that every failure promised an even more glorious outcome."

"By stealing the work of a brilliant mind?"

"You are so naive to hold the Professor in such high estimation. His resume is filled with a string of failures. I made sure of that. He is so inferior to my genius. Less than a fortnight ago, he thought he had found the cure for Melody's ills. He administered the antidote to her, but it only resulted in the acceleration of her symptoms promising certain death. Little did he know I tampered with his formula to guarantee failure."

"Are you mad? You purposely sabotaged his effort to cure Melody?"

"If he cured her, she would owe me nothing. I would not be able to win her."

"You're insane! Toying with Melody's life!"

"Once I take the EAS and turn myself into a Super-Emoticon and save her, she will gladly take my side to rule the world."

"You're a monster!"

"Time itself shall receive a new designation. It will no longer be divided by B.C. or A.D. Rather, it will be separated by 'B.S.' and 'A.S.' – 'Before Stu.' 'Anno Stu.'"

"Then what did you need me for? If the plan all along was for you take the solution?"

"Believe it or not, Melody, you, and I, are bound by a unique commonality. The three of us, on this entire island nation, are the only ones with the rare Hh blood type. Unfortunately, my blood and Melody's blood contain too many contaminants. I have suffered three unsuccessful experiments already and I am in dire straits. Melody's blood is also contaminated due to the CME debacle, and the antidote backlash. You are the only one who has the pure quality blood required for the success of the EAS."

"That's why you took my blood sample. You wanted to see if it was good enough for you to rob it from me!"

"Consider it your contribution to science. Of course I will ensure your obscurity by eliminating all mention of your participation in this earth-shattering, world-changing experiment."

47   TIME'S TAKE

At first, Les wanted to lash out at Stu with abominable expletives. But then he realized that donating his blood to Stu was the only way to assist in the success of EAS. As much as he hated Stu, Stu did have the same intention as Les. And that was to save Melody's life. That's what mattered most. If Les had to give his life, through his blood, to save Melody's life, then so be it. It was an absolutely worthy reason to die. What more could one ask for than to die for Melody? His original quest was to not die an ignoble, anonymous, meaningless death. And now that initial intention was being fulfilled. It was not how he had imagined it, but he could not fault fate for delivering on his desire by its own design rather than his.

Les saw by the digital readout that he had already lost two pints of blood. He quieted himself and closed his eyes, imagining a wholly healed Melody, who could recite her own A-B-C's, and deliver a soliloquy on the multiplication table. He wished he could bequeath Nameless Beach to her. He regretted not ever having made out a will. With his recent preoccupation with death and the Blue Sleep, why had he not thought of it? Although Melody had never actually used the word "love" he knew he felt it from her. So he had his Serena, his Blossom, his Angela. His very own Melody. It was a fine way to end his life. He felt unspeakable gratitude for the fullness that had come upon his life through Melody. It was only fitting that he should give his life for hers.

He opened his eyes to see three pints of blood had now flowed out from his body.

"How are you doing Mr. Nobody?" Stu asked.

Les felt no inclination to reply. He felt weak, not at all like himself, and far away from Nameless Beach.

"Your end marks my true beginning. Of course, I thought my beginning was to have taken place a long time ago, when I was in the prime of my youth, on the verge of winning the Mr. Universe Body Building Title. Coming in second place two previous times, I nearly gave up. But then I found out about the Professor's QLEF elixir. I knew that was going to be the answer to my dreams, the missing magic bullet that would give me the needed edge. I befriended Lydia, one of the Professor's graduate assistants, and made her mine. She was supposed to procure the solution for me secretly. But on the day of the monumental experiment, instead of doing as I instructed her, she made a last minute decision to take only a portion of the solution, thinking it would be easier to cover up her theft. Needless to say, without one hundred per cent potency, the formula was useless. It not only played havoc with my Hh blood type, it created other complications, resulting in the paralysis of my legs. That was a dark time for me. I never forgave Lydia for her failure. And I made sure she paid the price. After that was taken care of, I received an inquiring call from Medley, from Mexico. I realized then that the fates had an even greater destiny for me. That body building title was a trifle compared to the glorious future awaiting me. Indeed I would become a true Mr. Universe—Master and Commander of the entire world. And so I journeyed to Mexico and enlisted my service to the Professor to prod him on with a new formula."

"You killed Lydia," Les said, his horror providing the impetus to speak, despite his fading strength.

"It was a predetermined outcome. Her usefulness had been spent. She failed in her life's only service, which was to facilitate my rise to stardom."

"Who else have you killed?" Les could barely maintain his presence of mind to mouth the words. It was only the force of his outrage that fueled his will to speak. "Medley? The twins?"

"I am the chosen one. No one comes before me. The twins were threatening to steal my spotlight on the world stage. I could not allow that. I was guided by the hands of fate to design their demise."

Les was sickened by the revelation. After a long history of criminal acts of murder and deceit, how could Les trust Stu to do the best for Melody?

He had to believe that fate could not be so cruel, that it would respond with some offering of grace to spare her, and provide a future she deserved.

Les managed to muster just enough effort to take another look at the measuring instrument. Almost four pints of blood had been drained. It was an effort to maintain consciousness. A part of him wanted to stay awake, to be aware, while another part of him simply wanted to let go, and give in to the tempting call of sleep. His last thought before giving way was that he knew who he was. He was the one who loved Melody. That's all he needed to know about himself. That's all he wanted Melody to know about himself. By loving her he had defined himself. She was his deliverance. If only she were here that he could tell her so.

He closed his eyes.

48 DO RE MI

What happened next seemed to happen in another time and place. Actually Les was not sure it was happening at all. Perhaps he was dreaming it. But it did not have the closeness, the intimacy, of a dream. He felt quite separate from what was happening. And yet, he was also at the epicenter of storming events. The sensation of being a participant and a distant observer meshed and coalesced in and out upon the other.

"What's going on here?" It was the outraged voice of Melody.

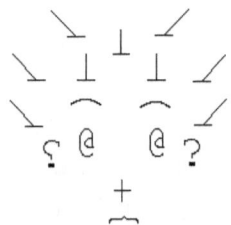

Stu replied in a pleading tone, "It's all for your sake, my lovely, my sweet."

"You sick swine! I know you're up to no good!"

Les managed to open his eyes and watched with rolling eyes, his vision intermittently going out of focus, as Melody struggled with Stu to remove the in-going intravenous tube from Stu's arm.

"Listen, my flower, please," Stu pleaded. "You

don't understand. Let me explain."

She withdrew the tube from his one arm and pushed him off the power chair onto the floor. Then she turned to Les and removed the tube extracting his blood, and put a bandage upon it.

"I have the EAS!" Stu cried out. "There in the refrigerator. As soon as I partake of it, I will be able to save you!"

"No. No more formulas. No more serums and potions and elixirs. No more experiments!" She went into the refrigerator, retrieved the sealed jar of EAS and smashed it on the floor.

"Noooooo!" Stu screamed.

Melody went back to tend to Les.

Stu in the meanwhile crawled towards Melody, dragging his paralyzed legs. Then he took out the other needle from his arm, aiming to stab Melody from behind. He lunged for her, while crying out, "I have a destiny!"

Melody turned around in time to kick Stu in the face. He fell back, blood continuing to flow out of both his arms.

Melody stepped back to care for Les again. "You must be Hh," she mumbled, more to herself than Les.

Les had no strength to make any kind of an acknowledging reply.

She put a clip on the tube to stop the outflow of blood and attached a new clean needle, inserting it into Les's other arm.

"I am meant for greatness!" Stu insisted. Then he speared a pair of scissors at Melody, wounding her arm.

She turned around to face Stu, who proclaimed "You can't foil my future!"

Melody let out a horrendous primal scream and upturned the power chair upon Stu, pinning him to the floor. "I can't breathe," Stu groaned. "Help me, I can't breathe!" He struggled to free himself, but to no avail.

Melody ignored his plea and slapped a bandage over the puncture on her arm. Then she removed all the restraints from Les.

By then all movements from Stu's lifeless body had ceased.

Melody removed the first tube from Les's arm. She attached a new needle and inserted it into her arm. Her blood was now flowing up into the monitor and back down into Les. She was replenishing his body with her blood, but there was no other source from which she could replenish her blood. She lay down on the bed beside him.

"Everything is going to be all right," she said. "Just remember I love you." She stroked his face. "I know I wasn't supposed to come until you told me, but I couldn't wait. I had to see you. I didn't want to spend another minute without you."

It was the first time she had used the word "love" and it brought tears to his eyes. As he struggled to keep his focus and maintain consciousness, Les managed to whisper slowly, "The EAS. Stu was going to save you."

"Hush. No need to talk. You save your strength. I don't know how much longer you will have, with my imperfect blood. Two or three months. Maybe six. It's not much, but it's all I have.

And I'm happy to know I'm giving you my all. Probably my forgetting as well. So if one day, you can't say your A-B-C's, or sing your do-re-mi's, you can blame it on me. Sorry I can't take the bad parts out. But that's why I love you so much. You always took in all my bad parts."

Then she gave him a long enduring kiss.

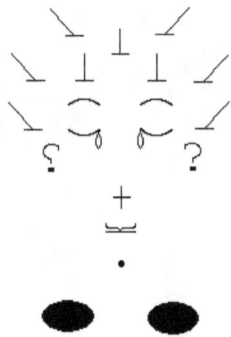

And Les succumbed to sleep, feeling the gentle stroke of her hand upon his face.

When Les awoke next, he did not know whether it was morning or afternoon or even what day. On the one hand it felt as if he had slept for days. But it also felt as if he had merely shut his eyes a moment ago.

Then he became aware of the sound of weeping. He also felt a great weight upon him. He opened his eyes to see Melody's body over his, and Yolanda and Esmeralda bent over atop Melody. He closed his eyes again, reassured by their muffled sobbing. It was a comforting sound, almost like a lullaby. It felt as if the three of them were embracing him.

49   UNCHANGED CHANGE

Melody's funereal took place at Nameless Beach. It was a great gathering. It included not only the small circle of people Les knew, but a large number of regular and occasional customers from the Medley Cafe, not to mention the owners and staff of businesses who were clients of the Medley Muffin Company. Les was quite surprised by the large turnout. He was humbled by and grateful for, all those there.

After the funereal, he planted lilies all around Melody's grave, so that it became a garden. He also successfully petitioned to have Nameless Beach changed to Melody Beach. Realizing he had only a limited time to live, he set out writing down Melody's story and how her love had changed him by showing him he had no need to change after all. Acceptance in itself, was the greatest change. He had in fact, become changed by not changing.

Through Melody's love, he had come to stop despising himself, to belittle himself, to berate himself. Through Melody's love, he had come to see he was worthy of being loved. Before Melody, he had been chasing a phantom dream to become a glorious figure who could accomplish some vague deeds of renown. All that was beside the point now. He could put his effort into something more worthwhile. And that was the telling of Melody's story.

Although Melody herself had told Les he

would only have perhaps half a year at most to live, an entire year went by as he lost himself in the writing of his book about her. And it took many months more before it was published. Then another year until it achieved respectable sales figures. He continued to live several more years after the initial successful reception of the book. And then came the invitation to participate as a member of the "retrospective" panel of writers on the literary outing of that ill-fated cruise ship.

As it turned out, there was a young and struggling, frustrated writer who sabotaged the ship with strategically placed bombs, setting them off simultaneously with his suicide vest of explosives, while ranting viciously at the gallery of authors of note. Les Dan Nil managed to escape the ship before its sinking and came to find himself alone at sea, with that one copy of his book, until he chanced upon my skiff.

50 RETURN OF THE I

When I awoke, I felt the wind. It was sunrise. I saw Les lying at my feet, completely still. He had passed away during my sleep. With my focus on my own pain and suffering, it had not occurred to me that Les might be the first of the two of us to die.

Even though initially I had resentfully posed as an anonymous wall of ears during his story telling, I had become ensnared and engaged in the accounting of his past. And I was deeply wounded by the sight of his lifeless figure. I trusted his soul was somewhere reunited with Melody. I didn't believe in the afterlife, but I wished it for him.

Somehow I found enough strength to set his body into the sea. I felt a eulogy was in order, but my parched throat was swollen shut. As I watched his body slip under water, I barely managed to whisper, "Do re mi, Les. Do re mi." That was the extent of my mourning statement. Then I collapsed back into the skiff, content to feel the breeze pass by softly.

After a period of rest, still feeble and weak and delirious, I knew I had to answer the call of the wind, rather than my original call to disappear at sea. It was the call of Serena, Blossom, Angela and Melody. Their names were in the wind.

I managed to hoist the jib sail and set the main sail and looked to the sun to point myself due west. As luck would have it, as if to promise the call answered to One-Eyed, Sir Wintry, Tip Top and

Les, by the end of the day, I sighted a cruise ship and was rescued.

After my recovery, when I was asked how I managed to survive my ordeal, I never mentioned Les, or his story of Melody and the other emoticons. I didn't want to be considered a deranged victim of some hallucination. But I knew it was Les and his storytelling that had kept me alive. It was the will to know what happened next, in order to arrive at the final outcome, that had urged me on.

And in the presence of another being, I was being recognized. My name mattered again. Not to Les who never found out. But to me. I would have shouted it out if I could have. My sense of self was reborn, however frail and weak, because of Les's appearance. I was engaged in the life of another, which reengaged me into mine. It was the return of my "I."

I regret having tossed Les's book into the ocean. I wish I had it now. But then again, perhaps because I didn't have the book, the story has been more strongly imprinted in my memory.

I no longer lament over my lost days of young glory. I'm past trying to reclaim my former identity. I have forgiven my parents. I am on healing terms with them.

So who am I now? No matter, as the Professor would assert. The question begs to be devalued. I'm not here to make a mark in the world, but to render my surrender to the Big Number; to feel the zap, get charged, and vent my fervent fever that I may qualify to a potential sum by fusing to my convergent courting current. If fortune smiles upon me, I'll catch a dream from the fall of stars and someone like Serena, Blossom, Angela, or Melody, will come in to my life.

And though I may suffer heartbreak that fell upon One-Eyed , Sir Wintry, Tip Top and Les, I'm willing to take on the coyotes of chance. Fifty-fifty seem fair odds to me. After all, life doesn't owe me anything. I'm the one who has an indebtedness to life.

As for the girl of my dreams, I may meet her one day in a cafe serving muffins. I may find her at a beach throwing flowers into the sea. I may look up into a tree house in the forest and see her sitting on a swing.

And after we come to know each other, she may even ask me to recite the multiplication table at night as we lie together under the stars. And as she drifts off to sleep in my arms, I will say her name to confirm my own. Through her I will know myself. Then in the morning, we will face the show of the sun as it rises, in the fulfillment of its infinite reprise.

THE END

ABOUT THE AUTHOR

Robert Yoshibo Shell was born in Okinawa, Japan.
Most of his life has been spent in the United States.
For a time he was stationed in Germany, then
studied in France. He travels to the Greek Islands
as often as he can. Currently he resides in Norway.